Secrets in Little Valley

The Amish Lantern Mystery Series
Book 2

By Mary B. Barbee

This is a work of fiction. All of the characters, organizations, and events portrayed in this novel are either products of the author's imagination or are used fictitiously.

Editing Team: Jenny Raith, Molly Misko, Julie Rietze, and Laura Fry

Cover Design by Daniela Colleo of Stunning Book Covers

www.marybbarbee.com

For Julie, who I have always trusted to keep my secrets.

For nothing is hidden that will not become evident, nor anything secret that will not be known and come to light.

Luke 8:17

Chapter One

"I'm so excited," Beth squealed as she reached across the table and squeezed Anna's arm. Anna stopped writing for a moment to look at her twin sister. Anna chuckled, her lips spreading into a wide grin. Ever since they were little, Beth would get so excited about planning a party. Although the actual social gathering would always cause her anxiety as the event approached, it was all the little details that she really enjoyed planning.

Beth struggled as a high-functioning autistic for many years. Whenever needed, her twin sister, Anna, would slide right into care-taking mode. Anna watched for signs that

Beth was feeling anxious in crowds and pulled her away for a few minutes. She pointed out to Beth when she had become overly obsessed about something, and she had grown to understand that some of Beth's habits were just part of their lives together.

"Yes, these are definitely exciting times. We have so much to thank Gotte for, after all this community has been through." Anna tried not to think much about how just a few weeks before, her son-in-law had been arrested for a crime he hadn't committed, and how terrifying all of it had been for the entire family. She was so grateful for his freedom and the powerful bond that Moses and her daughter, Sarah, shared - it had surely helped them through the hard times.

Moses was such a good man. Even though he had only been free for a day, he spent hours in his barn carving the most beautiful cherry wood cane for Anna. Since the accident, Anna couldn't walk without help, and Moses's wonderful gift allowed her the independence she craved.

A knock at the door from the other room interrupted Anna's thoughts, and she took note that Beth quickly jumped up to see who was there. My, how she has changed, thought Anna. Beth suffered from autism and would typically be the last to answer the door, but things were different now. She seemed more confident, more brave, since the traumatic events from a few weeks ago. Even though Anna suffered physically, Beth recovered quickly and naturally fell into caretaker mode for her twin sister.

Anna felt a pit in her stomach as she recalled the fear she felt that day. Desperately trying to clear Moses' name, the sisters had found themselves face-to-face with a killer. Thankfully, their efforts had helped solve the murder, and the killer was arrested, but the entire experience shook the community to the core. Little Valley was recovering and Beth and Anna hoped that the celebration would bring some focus back to the happiness and comfort that Little Valley had once offered their loved ones.

Anna's oldest daughter, Sarah, walked into the kitchen, her pregnant belly entering at least 12 inches ahead of her. "Daughter! What a lovely surprise! How are you feeling? Come sit down," Anna said. Sarah graciously took a seat in the chair next to her mother, leaning back slowly to allow room for the precious baby she was carrying. Her hands instinctively caressed her stomach.

Beth brought a small upholstered footstool from the living room, propping Sarah's feet on the stool while removing her slippers. She placed a handmade quilt around her shoulders to keep her warm. The temperature had dropped with the threat of winter starting, and the house held a chill that the small wood stove couldn't seem to keep at bay that day. Normally, the twins would have the house warmed from the hours of baking in the ovens, but they had decided their stock of baked goods was sufficient for the upcoming farmers' market scheduled for the weekend ahead. During the colder months, they typically sold less, and they especially welcomed the break this year.

"I'm exhausted. I've been having a few cramps off and on this morning, and the smallest things just take so much energy. How are you, Maem?" Sarah touched Anna's damaged knee gently.

"Oh, I'm fine! The English doctor says I will be ready to get back to my morning walks with Eli in just a couple weeks," Anna winked at Sarah.

"No, she won't, Sarah," said Beth firmly. "She will do no such thing. The doctor says her knee is healing nicely, but I think we'll be playing it safe for a while, especially with the cold season. You know how our bones can start to hurt at this age."

Anna waved her hand in the air as if Beth was overreacting.

"On the contrary! I'll be turning 60 years old before I know it, so I've got to keep my heart pumping," Anna said. She knew Beth meant well, but Anna didn't like being told what she could not do - and she also knew that Beth was fully aware of that.

Beth rolled her eyes and turned away to tend to the tray of teacups and cookies she was organizing for the three ladies to enjoy.

"You have three years to go, still, Maem, and you could use the rest," Sarah said, with a serious look directed at her mother.

"Denki, Sarah, but you don't need to worry about me," Anna said, looking over at her daughter. She adored Sarah and was so proud of the woman she had become. "Tell me about your cramps. Do you think you will have the baby today?" She reached over and touched Sarah's protruding belly with care, feeling for movement.

"The doctor says the baby could arrive anytime, but the first two babies were both so late in arriving. I think we still have a couple more weeks to wait," Sarah said.

Beth laid the tray down on the table next to Anna and in front of Sarah. "Well, we just need to make sure you're going to be feeling well in time for the celebration! I wouldn't mind holding my niece while you and Moses relax and enjoy all that we have prepared for you."

"Did you two hear about Matthew, Moses's best friend from childhood? He has requested to return to the community. If you remember, he did not return after his Rumspringa. He has been living in the nearby town of Springston, but he came to visit after hearing about Moses' arrest. I think he must have realized that he had made a mistake leaving the community. He has requested forgiveness from the bishop and the elders." Sarah spoke, the words stumbling out of her mouth between brief breaks here and there as if she were feeling a bit out of breath.

"That's glorious news!" Beth exclaimed. "I had hoped and prayed for so many years that he would return. If the elders approve, then we will have reason to celebrate both Moses and Matthew's return home! Gotte is gut!"

"Yes, that is so wonderful," Anna agreed, "and speaking of the party, I'm so excited to tell you all about the delicious food we have on the menu. Let's start with the dessert, my favorite, of course." Anna smiled at Beth. "We are baking three of your grandmother's famous cherry cobblers. And at least 3 batches of the sugar cookies. We'll need to borrow your glass cookie jars, if you don't mind. Our cookie jars are all reserved and used for transporting the goods to the market on the weekends." Getting lost in the list in front of her, Anna didn't notice right away that Sarah's breathing had become heavier.

"Maem," Sarah said as a whisper before taking another deep breath, "I think... I'm having the baby." Her face was flushed, her eyes filled with a unique mix of excitement and pain.

"Ach du lieva!" Beth cried out, jumping up to run by Sarah's side.

"Beth, dabber schpring and tell Eli to get the buggy ready! We're having a baby!!"

Chapter Two

———◆◆◆———

Where is she? Levi asked himself, pacing up and down the riverbed. To reduce his anxiety, he sat down next to the stream. His reflection floated along the surface of the water, slightly warped by the gentle current. Levi Mast had just turned fifteen. He still had what his mother would call 'baby fat' on his oval, boyish face. His eyes were bright and his nose was perfectly straight. It was getting easier and easier to see his father's face in his image each day that Levi grew older. He was finally growing a bit taller, and he hoped that he would be as tall as his father when he reached the other side of puberty. Levi rubbed

his arms, tanned from the long hours of working outside under the sun on his family farm, and looked
around, searching for a sign of Ruby.

His concern for her absence increased. Levi called
out Ruby's name. Sometimes they would play games
where one or the other would hide, but he was sure she
wouldn't have carried on for this long. *Maybe she is confused about where or when we were supposed to meet,* he
thought to himself, although he knew that was unlikely
since they always met at their secret spot around the
same time every other afternoon. Between the stream
and the tall trees, Levi had formed a heart shape with a
collection of rocks he had found and brought to their
favorite spot. Ruby had thought this gesture was so
romantic. Levi remembered her beautiful smile and the
excitement he felt when she jumped into his arms the
first time she noticed the rock pattern he had created.

He was usually the one that was late, and this day was
no different. Some days it was difficult for Levi to get away
with all the work that he had on his plate. He helped his
father on the family farm and in the small corner store that
his father built to sell their farm's bounty of produce. On
busy days, as soon as he could get away, Levi would run like
lightning to find Ruby sitting patiently next to the "heart

rocks." But today, she wasn't there to greet Levi, and he had a strange feeling about it.

He shook his head as he pushed the feelings away. Maybe he was just feeling guilty for being late again - especially since Ruby never gave him a hard time about it. She was always so positive and light-hearted. She was such a joy to be around and when he was away from her, he counted the minutes until they could be together again. Levi knew they were young, but he could not imagine life without her.

Ruby also loved this special spot and their time together, almost as much as Levi did. She was younger than Levi - only 18 months younger, at thirteen years old, but she wanted to take things slow and avoided talking about the future too much. She knew she wanted to explore the world outside of Little Valley just as her older sister had, but Levi was set on staying home. He wasn't even sure if he was interested in experiencing Rumspringa. Ruby wanted to explore, and she longed for the day when Rumspringa would finally be in front of her. Her sister had decided not to return to the community for baptism after Rumspringa, and her parents were heartbroken to learn of her decision. Ruby wasn't sure she would follow in her sister's footprints exactly, but she was eager to find out why Esther had chosen the path she did.

All the same, Ruby thought it was exciting to meet Levi in private. Only her closest friend, Grace, knew about their secret meetings. She told Grace all of her secrets, and she fully trusted that Grace wouldn't tell anyone else. The two of them had been best friends and neighbors all of their lives, and they had built a bond that was unbreakable.

The young lovers knew that their secret love affair, as innocent as it was, would bring so much shame to their families if revealed -especially since Ruby's father was the bishop in the community. They were far too young to be dating. Regardless, Ruby didn't care. And neither did Levi. They couldn't stay away from each other, and they were willing to risk it all just for those fleeting moments in their secret space by the stream in the woods.

Levi decided that he would give Ruby a few more minutes before heading home. Maybe it wasn't as late as he thought it was, or maybe *she* was the one that was running late this time. Ignoring his sixth sense nagging him, he allowed his thoughts to wander back to when he first met Ruby. Levi had a tough time trusting girls and falling in love since his first experience. Two years before, when he was twelve, Colette, the beautiful blonde girl who lived next door broke his heart. The experience hardened him and made him wary to even look at another girl for a while. He knew he had plenty of time for love and romantic relationships later in his life. But, he met Ruby at a wedding celebration held in the community, and anyone could immediately see that she was by far the most beautiful girl in the community. When he asked about her, his older brother quickly let him know that she was the bishop's daughter and shouldn't be approached. His friends all talked about befriending her but none mustered the courage to actually do so. Levi was intrigued.

One day, as if it were fate, Ruby hand delivered a message from the bishop to his father's farm when his parents were at the market and he was alone. He was struck by how beautiful and articulate she was. The two young teens spent the next hour - almost two - chatting, laughing, and flirting with each other. It felt so comfortable and natural. It surprised him when it came time for her to leave, and he felt the urge to not let her go. She told him later that she felt the same. After that day, Levi couldn't stop thinking about Ruby. He would find excuses to sneak around the church or any other place he suspected Ruby might be.

Soon after, he ran into her in the town and walked her home. And then that soon became more and more common. Ruby feared their appearance in town might become suspicious, and loving the excitement of it all, she suggested they meet in the woods by the stream. And it was history from there.

Dusk was settling, and the sun was playing hide and seek between the tall peaks of the trees. Levi guessed he must've been waiting for an hour or more now, and he was stricken with worry. He had to leave and head home, but he was conflicted. He didn't want to go without seeing Ruby, but he told himself that the only explanation was that something important must've come up.

With a sigh, Levi decided he would have to wait until their next meeting to find out. He headed home with his head hanging low.

Chapter Three

It was another beautiful day in Little Valley. The sky was a brilliant color blue, and the trees were almost bare. The air was still, leaves lay scattered on the ground-their once vibrant colors turned dingy. The temperatures were dropping, and if these weren't all clear signs that autumn was turning into winter, the decrease in the tourist boom served as a solid reminder instead.

Mark Streen sat on the front porch outside the sheriff's office, drinking his first cup of steaming black instant coffee. He was new to the position of Mainstay County Sheriff, recently appointed by the County Commission to take the seat until the next election, and he welcomed the peace and quiet on the outskirts of Little Valley, where the sheriff's office sat.

Derek McCall had been serving as Sheriff for almost a decade before him, and since they had falsely accused a local Amish shop owner of McCall's murder, Mark knew that he had a big job ahead of him when it came to making amends with the community. He was up for the challenge. As a Christian himself, he admired the Amish and their disciplined lifestyles, so when he was approached with the opportunity to protect and serve Little Valley, he immediately started a plan in motion. His plan not only included helping these folks rebuild the trust in lawmen over the next 10 months, but he was hoping to establish a relationship that would then lead to an election win, when the time came. He had always wanted to live out in this area, and he felt blessed to have received the call.

Sheriff Streen was set to interview an officer that morning for the deputy role, and he was looking forward to it. The candidate was a young man, but eager to relocate, as well. He had served temporarily in this office recently, covering weekend shifts, and he was also looking for a long-term position, working closely with the community.

After what these people have been through, I can't imagine much more could happen, thought Mark, as he finished the last sip of coffee. He rose to his feet, and with perfect timing, the expected young man pulled up to the station in an older white Toyota pickup truck. Seeing the Sheriff standing outside, he didn't waste time. Dressed in full uniform, the junior officer jumped out of the driver's side of the truck, and hurried to the porch, energetically hopping up the steps. He couldn't be a day older than eighteen, Mark thought. The young man was thin and lanky, with traces of acne on his cheeks and dirty blond hair, styled in a crew-cut with a little too much hair gel. He stretched out his arm, a wide smile across his face.

"Good morning! You must be Sheriff Streen. It's a pleasure to meet you. The name's Chase Brown." The Sheriff shook his hand and returned the greeting. They exchanged niceties: the sheriff asking how Chase's trip went, Chase asking how the sheriff's day was going. Holding the door open, Mark invited Chase to have a seat in the front office.

"Ah, it's good to be back," Chase said. "It really feels homey in here.. and out there, too," Chase pointed out the window, referring to the town.

The sheriff's office was an old small house refurbished about twenty years ago. What used to be the living room was the front office, holding two desks - one twice as big as the other, but each with older vinyl covered office chairs. The wheels on the chairs felt as if they were tired and didn't wish to roll on the hardwood floorboards, and they grunted when the chair moved even the tiniest bit. In the corner of the front office were two additional upholstered "visitor chairs." The cushions on the chairs, once white floral patterns but now gray, did not extend to the backs of the chairs and there were no armrests, but it made little sense to replace the chairs over the years since visiting the Sheriff's Office was so rare.

The former kitchen remained in use as the small kitchen for the Sheriff's Office, but instead of canned foods, flour, and pasta, the cabinets were filled with coffee grounds, artificial sweetener and ramen noodles. There was a steel door in the kitchen that looked out of place, leading to the area where the home's single bedroom had been refashioned into a single holding cell. It sat empty of prisoners and only contained an old bunk bed with uncovered mattresses that had yellowed over the years. A small stained sink and toilet were also crammed in the small space.

Standing in the front office, you could easily see back to the empty cell since the steel door was propped open. Chase glanced back there briefly and said offhandedly, ". ..first time seeing that empty."

"I can't imagine it has had many occupants," the Sheriff responded. "Let's have a seat. I just have a few questions for you. I won't keep you long."

Chase nodded, took a seat, checked to make sure he had turned off his cell phone, and met Mark's gaze. He knew eye contact was important in an interview and he really wanted to make a good impression. "Well, first of all, let me say, thank you for the opportunity to interview. I'm glad to be here, and I am very interested in working with you."

Mark thought that sounded a little rehearsed, but he made a mental note that Chase was making a decent effort. "Good, so, how long have you been working with the police department? And why do you want to transition to a deputy role?" Mark knew there wouldn't be much action in Little Valley and wanted to make sure that this young man wasn't expecting that.

"Well, to be honest, I only just started on the police force out east. I'm looking for a place to start my career, a position where I can learn. I want to work in a community setting where I can get to know the town and the people in the town. I want them to see me and feel safe. And I want to find a place to make my home. I don't have any family - both my parents passed away when I was young, and I floated around the foster care system in the Nashville area for all my upbringing. I want stability and when I was assigned temp duty here a few weekends ago, I got to meet some citizens of Little Valley. And I don't know, it just felt right." Chase paused. He realized that he had been talking a lot and he searched the Sheriff's face to see if he had become disinterested.

The Sheriff liked everything he was hearing, but he wanted to keep a poker face in front of Chase. "What do you think you bring to this position and what are your expectations? I want to make sure we're on the same page."

Without hesitation, Chase responded, "I am willing to learn whatever you'll teach me, sir," he made a point to call Sheriff Streen the respectful name to give the impression that he would stay in line. "I want you to trust me to have your back, and lean on me for help when, and if you need it. I think you and I could make a great team, to be blunt. I am easy to work with. I'm eager. I know my place and I'm good at following direction..." Chase stopped talking abruptly. He knew that this had taken a weird turn. It almost sounded like he was begging for the job - which he probably would, if asked - but he also didn't want to taint the good impression he had started with just a few minutes earlier. "I'm just driven, sir. I want the job and I believe I'm the right one for it."

Sheriff Streen held up his hand and lowered his head slightly as if to politely silence young Chase. He could tell that the young man really wanted the job, and he liked the idea of having someone completely green in the position.

Mark found working with younger mentees refreshing. He had never worked with someone quite this young, but there is nothing worse than having to work day in and day out with someone who thinks they know better than you and constantly tries to challenge you. He looked forward to having someone he could teach and mold. "When can you start?" Mark stood and stretched out his hand as a sign of an official offer.

Chase couldn't hide his excitement. He jumped up, almost knocking over the visitor chair, and responded, "Seriously? I got the job?"

"Well, as long as you're ok with the pay and..." Mark paused briefly and looked around, "and the boredom, then, yes, you've got the job."

"I'll take it," Chase smiled from ear to ear. Everything was falling into place just as he had hoped.

Chapter Four

A nna leaned on her cane and watched Eli and Noah as they moved the large mahogany table towards the wall of windows in Beth's living room. "Please make sure it's centered," she directed. Anna wasn't able to help with the heavy lifting, but she was happy to serve as the director of the event instead. Beth buzzed around like a busy bee behind the men, moving the chairs into a large uneven circle on the outskirts of the living areas.

Little Valley was blessed with perfect temperatures for the day of the homecoming celebration. "It's like *Gotte* turned up the heat so we could enjoy the wonderful fresh air," Beth joked earlier. The day before, it felt almost like mid-winter, but on this day, no wool coats would be necessary. A cape would be comfortable enough.

Beth began placing the white cotton embroidered tablecloth on the table. "I love when we have reasons to use *Maem*'s beautiful tablecloth," she said. Her face was beaming with excitement.

"Yes, it is certainly beautiful," Anna agreed.

The front door was partially propped open, and Mr. Hatfield entered. "Excuse me, Mrs. Miller," Mr. Hatfield said politely, "I noticed the door was open."

"Ah, come in please.. you have perfect timing!" Anna greeted him. "How are you, Mr. Hatfield?"

Mr. Hatfield owned the flower shop next to Moses' hardware store, and when he got wind that the community was celebrating Moses' return home, he offered to provide the flower arrangements. The sisters only had plans to collect wildflowers, but graciously accepted Mr. Hatfield's gift.

"Fine, fine, thank you," said Mr. Hatfield, avoiding eye contact. He seemed a little on edge, nervous and uncomfortable, but the sisters knew that was normal demeanor for him.

"And how is your wife?" asked Anna. Mr. Hatfield's wife, Samantha Hatfield, kept to herself and had hardly ever spoken to either of the sisters despite the twins' effort to greet her upon meeting at the farmers' market or around town. The sisters were sure that Samantha did not have any friends here in Little Valley. They had only seen her alone or with Mr. Hatfield. She would always walk a step or two ahead of him when they were together.

"She is well, thank you. She sends her congratulations to Moses for his release and return home. We both knew that Moses was innocent of killing Sheriff McCall, and we are happy that the truth came to light. How is Moses? Is he here yet?"

"Ah, I'm afraid not yet, but he should be here soon if you'd like to wait with Eli and Noah outside," Anna replied. "Moses and his family are adjusting well to his return, thank you for the kind thoughts. Sarah, Moses' wife, just had her third baby, you know. She is such a good baby. Everyone is happy and well."

"That is good to hear," Mr. Hatfield said. "A new baby must be very exciting. Mrs. Hatfield and I were never able..." He stopped in mid-sentence and shifted his eyes to the table in front of the window. He cleared his throat and took a step towards the table. "Shall I set these flowers here?" he asked. Without waiting for a response, he set the carefully arranged flowers down in the center of the table.

The beautiful mix of white, blue and yellow shades looked perfect against the elegant tablecloth.

"Oh! They look so beautiful!," Beth exclaimed, holding her hands in front of her as if in prayer.

"Thank you so much, Mr. Hatfield," the sisters said in unison. It wasn't uncommon for the twins to finish each other's sentences or to say the same thing at the same time, and most of the time they didn't even realize it happened.

Mr. Hatfield nodded, "You're welcome. Good day, now. I should get back to the shop. Please tell Moses I said hello and to stop by the next time he is at the store."

"I'll pass the word along," Anna said as he turned toward the door to leave. "Have a wonderful weekend," she called out.

Before returning her attention to setting up the party, Anna said a silent prayer for Mr. Hatfield and his wife to find happiness. She had a sinking feeling that joy was missing from their lives, and she prayed for positive change.

Beth meticulously arranged the sisters' beautiful baked goods on the table, lining the dishes up so they created a symmetrical pattern. Beth's autism took over when she was working on anything that required attention to detail, but the results were flawless. Anna attributed Beth's perfectionism to create refined and delicious cookies and bread to their success in business. The careful details on each pie, cobbler, loaf of bread, and cookie made it nearly impossible for anyone to pass their booth at the farmers' market without stopping to look at what was laid out on the table.

Next to the baked goods laid teacups, a pot of hot coffee, glasses, and a pitcher of water. Just as Beth laid out the small set of dessert plates made of china, the guests started to arrive. The large living room and dining room areas began to feel a bit smaller, as the community gathered. The men entered to grab a quick drink and a bite to eat and then headed outside to the large porch while the room filled with the women's chatter.

The women of the community cooed over Sarah's new baby, Rosemary. Anna checked in on Mary, a young woman who had come to her a few weeks before distraught over feelings she had for a man that she wasn't sure loved her back. "How are you, Mary?" asked Anna, warmly.

"I'm doing so good, Mrs. Miller, thank you so much for asking!" Mary responded, with a teacup in hand. "Luke is busy preparing his farm for the winter, but with Eli's mentoring, he is optimistic that Spring will bring healthy crops." Mary paused and lowered her voice to a whisper, "And, I think he might propose soon, too!" She smiled an impish grin.

"That's wonderful!" Anna responded, sincerely happy for Mary. Beth and Anna's younger sister, Susan soon interrupted their conversation.

"Anna, you have to tell me the secret to making your bread so fluffy. I know that you and I both use *Maem's* recipe, but I cannot make it rise like this no matter what I try!"

Beth overheard the conversation and quickly stepped in to be included. "Little sister, that is our best-selling product at the market. Are you sure you are using the right amount of salt?"

Anna spoke up speaking to both sisters, "Susan has the exact same recipe. It has to be the size of your pan, Susan. That really can make such a big difference."

The conversations among the women continued, while outside, the men discussed their plans for preparing their land and animals for the winter. Remarks about the odd weather were exchanged, and the discussion turned to business.

"How has business been, Cousin Moses?" asked Amos Troyer. Amos was Sarah's cousin, Beth's second oldest son. The circle of men turned their attention to Moses.

"Decent. Business is decent, with tourism settling down and all," Moses responded. There was still a sense of tension around Moses, for some of the community had fallen into the belief during his arrest that he was indeed guilty of killing Sheriff McCall. With his release and the discovery of the killer, there was a sense of embarrassment that remained in the air, like a gray cloud just before a thunderstorm. But Moses was a forgiving man, and he did not hold any grudges against anyone in the community. He was so grateful to be back home with his family and just in time for Rosemary's birth.

Eli was impressed with Moses' resilience, but he was conscious that it might still be tough to talk about it. Wanting to change the subject, he interjected, "I'll tell you what, just in the past few months, the tourism has really boomed, eh? I guess you all have heard about the bed-and-breakfast that is being built in town. And has anyone seen that drifter around? Where did he even come from? He gives me the creeps."

"I saw him walking out near your place, Bishop Pack er... just yesterday," said Christopher Yoder. Christopher was a thin, young unmarried man with a strong jawline and thick glasses that made his eyes seem small. "Did you interact with him?" Everyone's attention turned to the bishop who had been exceptionally quiet since he arrived.

It seemed as if Bishop Packer wasn't feeling well. He had indeed been trying to find a good time to exit the party early, but no one else knew how distracted he was. He and his wife, Margaret, had wanted to show their support for Moses, but they were secretly distraught because their daughter Ruby had not come home the night before.

"No, I didn't see anyone out of the ordinary," he responded, but he fought to keep his emotions hidden. For the first time, he wondered if Ruby could be in trouble. He had just assumed that Ruby was up to no good like her older sister, Esther, since their disagreement over breakfast. The bishop had assumed that she was staying away to punish him or make a point, and that she would return after she cooled off. But now he couldn't ignore the sick feeling that was forming in his stomach. Bishop Packer quickly excused himself and went inside to collect his wife.

Chapter Five

"Gimme another shot, Archer." Samuel Graber's words came out as a slur as he slid his empty shot glass down the bar towards the young bartender. Archer Melgren caught the glass swiftly and set it in the sink. He grabbed a clean shot glass and the nearby bottle of Jim Beam, pouring it expertly as if it was all one single action. Against the regulations, Archer never even closed the bottle when Samuel was sitting at the bar. Some nights he couldn't even keep up with the bar owner's refill requests and considering Samuel had a short temper - *and* Archer really needed the job - it could be a pretty stressful situation. Tonight Samuel seemed determined to drink the bar completely out of liquor. Archer may be young, but it was easy to sense something was bothering his boss.

"Wanna talk about it?" asked Archer. He was reluctant to open up the conversation, but it was practically expected of the bartender to lend an ear. Not only did he want to keep his job and give a good impression, but talking out problems with the customers just seemed like part of the job. And he was often told he was a good listener. There was no denying that some citizens of Little Valley saved a pretty penny by showing up to the pub for much needed "therapy." No appointment needed, of course.

Samuel grunted. "I'm mad as hell," he said as he slammed the empty shot glass down on the shiny cherry wood bar top. "That damned new sheriff in town is threatening to shut down the gaming in here. He says it's causin' problems in town. We all know that it's only causin' problems in that God-fearing community down the road. I make good money off those games and the games bring in the crowds. We're gonna end up in over our heads if he shuts down the tables."

As if on cue, a loud roar rose in the air from the rowdy group of regulars huddled in the corner of the dimly lit room. It was dusk, and the crowd that Samuel referred to hadn't yet arrived. There were three men and two women

- all very familiar faces to Archer - that had decided to spend their late Saturday afternoon together at the Little Valley pub. One of the men stood, dealing another round of cards, as the other players chattered incessantly about who *really* won the previous game, and who was going to win the next one. The games seemed pretty innocent to Archer- except for the occasional fights that resulted from too many drinks and too many losses.

Since he had started tending the bar about a year ago, he had seen a few Amish fellows wander in the bar sheepishly, usually very late at night, to try their hand at the game. They stood out like sore thumbs with their plain clothing and mannerisms. They never ordered drinks, and they were always more polite than the rest of the patrons. Samuel would always give them a hard time relentlessly during their visit, but he would never turn away a player with cash. Archer knew Samuel saw the Amish as easy targets in the game. Samuel had commented recently that he could afford the new car he wanted if he could just get more Amish to come play.

So, Archer was not fully surprised at the news that Samuel shared, but he still dared to play devil's advocate and defend the nice guys. "Did the sheriff say specifically that it's the Amish community that is the problem? I can't actually imagine he could shut it all down just because they asked for it."

Samuel looked at Archer with cold eyes and a clenched jaw. Archer took a step back and wished he could suck all the words he just uttered right back into his mouth. Archer berated himself silently and tried to regain his composure. *What was I thinking?!?* He stuttered, "I mean, you're probably right. I just..."

Samuel interrupted him with a loud slap on the bar that got everyone's attention. "What are you trying to say, boy? Are you on their side or mine?" Samuel's eyebrows furrowed over his eyes like dark thunderclouds and Archer could see spittle resting on his bottom lip. "Don't you work for me?" he asked the rhetorical question and then, his voice returning to his normal slur and tone, asked, "maybe you'd rather go work for those freaks? I'm sure they'd be happy to have you."

"That's not what I meant, Samuel, you're misunderstanding me," Archer said, trying to hide the disgust he felt for his boss. He felt his shoulders creep up to his ears and took a deep breath. "I was just trying to see if there might be another reason, so I could help you figure it out."

"That *is* the reason, kid" Samuel responded, spit flying in the air as he spoke the words. He swallowed the last bit of his beer, tipping the bottle back. Archer placed another shot in front of him with no coaxing this time. "The sheriff is trying to say that we're breaking county laws *and* he's accusing me of using the games to pad my own pockets. But I know he's just trying to get on *their* good side. After what happened when those idiots arrested that hardware shop owner, he thinks he can make it alright and get back in their favor. It's stupid and it's ridiculous. And I'm gonna fight it, I tell ya."

Archer, relieved to see that Samuel was slipping back into a more annoyed and less hostile mood, paused before saying, "You're probably right. Maybe I can talk to the sheriff and see if there's a license we're missing or something like that?"

"You must think I'm a fool," Samuel responded, jutting out his chin and rising to his feet. "I don't need some kid to save my bar. I'll deal with the sheriff and I'll deal with the Amish, too. It's time they learned a lesson about who owns this town. You just worry about serving drinks. And don't make me regret tellin' ya either." He turned and walked toward the obnoxious group of players at the old tattered poker table in the corner of the room.

"Nice talking to you," muttered Archer when Samuel was out of earshot. He shook his head as he gathered the empty beer bottle and shot glass and placed them in the sink. He grabbed the dingy rag out of the tub of bleach water, wrung it out, and proceeded to wipe down the bar. He tried to push any worries to the back of his mind, chalking up the experience as just another pointless conversation with just another drunk. But Samuel's threats replayed over and over again in his mind.

Chapter Six

The room was dark except for a small crack of dim light that shone from underneath the door on the adjoining wall. There was the faint sound of water dripping slowly, but no other noise could be heard. Ruby did not know where she was, but she knew she was in trouble. She remembered waiting for Levi in the woods. He was late again. When she had heard a noise, she thought Levi was playing their usual game, hiding in the trees. But then... tears trickled down her cheeks as she remembered how someone else had jumped out and grabbed her. The man had covered her mouth with a cloth. Everything went dark, and she couldn't remember anything else.

How long have I been here? Ruby thought. Without any windows, it was impossible to decipher what time of day it was. She had been taken from her and Levi's spot in the woods in the late afternoon just a couple hours before dinnertime. Surely her parents would be concerned when she didn't arrive for dinner, unless... Ruby shook her head, remembering how she had recently not come home for dinner. It was just last week. She and her father had argued over the house rules, again, and she had decided to teach him a lesson and hide at Grace's house for a few hours. She really just wanted to see if her father would even worry about her, or if he would prefer it if she weren't there. In the end, it was Ruby that snuck in the house after dark, stealing some bread and a couple cookies from the kitchen before slipping into bed. As far as she was concerned, her point was made. Her father worried about what other members of the community would think more than he cared for her feelings. Ruby was convinced that her older sister, Esther, had felt the same way. The next morning Ruby's father greeted her for breakfast, and they never spoke about the missed meal again. Oh, how Ruby regretted that now. Would he even know she was in serious trouble?

She blinked her eyes, trying desperately to accustom her eyes to the darkness. Trying not to panic, she decided to try to sit up and see if she could stand. She thought she saw what must be a door leading out of this horrible place. As she lowered her feet to the ground, she quickly realized she was barefoot. The floor was hard cold concrete, and she felt a cold band of metal around her right ankle. Reaching down, she realized she was chained to the bed. She gasped. Any attempt to remain calm was immediately forgotten.

She opened her mouth to call out for help, but her throat was dry - and it hurt terribly to swallow, much less to scream. Her mind was racing. She knew she had seen the man before, but she couldn't place where, or figure out who he was. She couldn't even see his face clearly in her mind. Her head was so foggy, she couldn't think.

Ruby swallowed again, and she raised her hands to rub the front of her neck instinctively. She was so thirsty, her tongue felt swollen, and her throat felt like it was on fire. *I need to get home*, Ruby thought, wringing her hands. Ruby was diagnosed with epilepsy when she was only five years old, and she feared she was going to need her medicine soon. She hated that she lived in fear of having a seizure day in and day out, but as she grew older, she had come to understand the importance of taking her medicine every day. As long as she took care of herself, there was less of a chance of her falling into an epileptic seizure.

Frantic, she began to feel around in the dark. The bed she was sitting on had an elaborate metal frame with a curved design on the headboard. Ruby ran her hands along the curves, and touched the cold hard wall behind the bed, feeling the lines and textures of a brick wall.

There was a small round wooden table sitting next to the bed. As she explored it with her fingers in the dark, she found only a plastic bottle sitting in the center. She thought it felt like the shape and the pliable plastic of a water bottle you might find at the general store, and she hoped she was right. She could hear the pop of the seal on the cap as she turned it. She lifted it to her mouth and drew comfort as the room temperature water soothed her throat. After a few swallows, she had some relief, but she soon realized she should probably be more conservative and save some water for later. After all, she had no idea where she was, if she would get more water, or if she was left to die.

She took a deep breath and tried to gather herself. Ruby closed the water bottle and set it back on the table. She laid back down and closed her eyes, steadying her rapid breathing. The mattress was actually very comfortable, more comfortable than her bed at home. Although her own bed was cozy enough, Ruby had never slept in such a soft bed as this. The sheets and heavy comforter smelled brand new. The new smell reminded her of the pastel pink sheets her *Maem* had given her for her birthday a couple years ago. She loved the way the new sheets smelled when she first opened the packaging. Wanting to preserve the scent, she had begged her *Maem* not to launder them.

Shaking her head, she sat up again, refusing to allow herself to feel comfortable. She needed to think. Her eyes had adjusted to the darkness a bit, and she could discern the shape of what looked like a cluttered workbench against the back corner of the room. There was a large utility sink just next to that, and what she had thought was a door, definitely was one. That appeared to be all there was in the room besides the bed and the small table next to her.

She could feel that she was wearing a long cotton gown. She believed it must be a nightgown, similar to the one she wore to bed each night. Her blonde hair was down and fell around her shoulders. She shuddered at the thought of someone else changing her clothes. Where were the shoes and clothes she was wearing when she was taken? Where was her *kapp*? Ruby was terrified.

She called out, "Hello?! Can anyone hear me? Please, I need help!" Her throat was feeling better from the water. She called out for help a few more times, but her voice seemed to evaporate in the damp heavy air. There was no response. No sound at all.

What am I going to do? Her heart raced. Realizing she was out of options, she decided she had better lay back down. She needed to stay calm and put together a plan. Ruby laid her head on the soft pillow and pulled the down feather cover up close to her face. Her eyelids felt heavy, so she gave in and closed her eyes. She began praying silently and drifted off to sleep.

What seemed to Ruby like only a minute later, she woke to the sound of a key unlocking the door. She began to tremble as a figure entered the room. A stream of light shone directly in Ruby's face instantly blinding her. She put her hands up as if to shield the light from her eyes and tried to see who was standing in front of her.

"How are you doing?" the male voice asked with a neutral tone.

Ruby didn't respond. She was overcome with fear. *This can't be real*, she thought.

"Listen, I know this is probably scary for you," he said again, in a matter-of-fact tone, "but you won't be down here for long."

The light continued to shine in Ruby's face. She lowered her hand and cast her eyes to the floor. Tears fell down her cheeks. Her body shook, and she wrung her hands, remaining silent.

The man shifted his weight to his left foot and said, "Well, like I said, this is only temporary. I just thought I'd check on you. I actually didn't expect you to be awake."

"What do you want from me? What are you going to do with me?" Ruby asked, her voice quiet and shaky, and her eyes still downcast.

"That's not actually up to me," he responded. Seeming suddenly frustrated, he quickly reached over and set down an extra bottle of water on the table next to her and briskly turned and left the room, locking the door behind him.

"Wait!" Ruby called out, "Wait! Please, come back! Please, you have to help me!!"

She heard another heavy door shut - maybe a few yards away - and then she found herself again sitting in silence and cloaked in darkness. Overcome with emotion, Ruby threw herself down on the pillows and sobbed loudly. *How could I have been so stupid to meet with Levi in the woods? Why couldn't I have been a better daughter and obeyed my parents? I wish so badly that I was with my mother right now, and even Dat.* As frustrating as her father could be, she would give anything to be sitting next to him, safe and sound at home.

Ruby's head was pounding, and she felt so tired. She could barely keep her eyes open, and her stomach grumbled from hunger. She wished more than ever that she had not left the breakfast table without eating that morning.

As tears streamed down her face, she closed her hands together in prayers of forgiveness and begged *Gotte* to save her. Once again, she drifted off to sleep.

Chapter Seven

Relaxing after the celebration, Noah and Eli were spending the afternoon taking advantage of the unusually warm temperatures, preparing their gardens for the upcoming colder months. Anna and Beth were sitting in Anna's living room, fabric laid across their laps. The sisters were busy sewing their latest quilting project. They were working on a traditional shadow box quilt with dark winter blues, greens and shades of gray, and were about a third of the way into the project. The hope was to finish the quilt before the holiday to give as a gift to Moses' childhood friend, Matthew. Matthew had left the faith during his *Rumspringa*, but was recently forgiven and permitted to return to the community after fifteen long years. He was a very close friend of Moses, and Moses had missed him terribly while he was away. All the men in the community were pleased that Matthew was back, and he was set to work with the others preparing the different community farms for the approaching winter. Matthew was a single man with an attractive, clean-shaven face, and there were more than a couple single women who wished he would look their way.

"The party was wonderful, wasn't it, Sister?" asked Beth, although she already knew Anna's answer.

"*Ja*, it was a blessing indeed," answered Anna without losing pace. Her threaded needle moved like steady waves in an ocean. The twins had sewed dozens of quilts in their lifetime together, and enjoyed the entire process from beginning to end. "Isn't baby Rosemary just as sweet as she can be? She is such a delightful baby."

"*Ach jah*, she is so fantastic! I am so grateful to see Sarah and Moses and their little family happy again" Beth said. Then, as if she just remembered something, she asked, "Have you heard anything about the new sheriff? I've only just heard he hired the young officer that worked on the weekends while Moses was…" She hesitated to even say the word, and she didn't have to - Anna knew what she meant.

"We should bring them some bread as a welcome gift," Anna responded.

Beth nodded in agreement. "*Ja*, *gute* idea, *schwester*."

Just then, there was a loud knock on Anna's heavy wooden front door. Anna was still relying on a cane to get around easily, so Beth quickly lifted her side of the quilt off her lap and set it down on the couch, careful to not let it touch the floor. She rose from her seat and called out, "coming!" as she proceeded toward the door.

Opening the door, Anna could hear Beth say, "Oh, *gute mariye*, Bishop Packer! Please come in. *Wie bischt*?"

Bishop Joseph Packer entered the living room with his head bare, straw hat in hand. He was a distinguished older gentleman with a long beautiful beard showing his many years of marriage and dedication to his kind wife, Margaret. Anna knew by the lack of color in his face and his worried expression that something was not right.

"*Hallo*, ladies," the bishop said as he nodded at each of them. "Thank you for your hospitality, but I'm afraid I am here for an urgent favor to ask of you."

"*Wilkumme*, Bishop, how can we help?" Anna asked. She had forgotten all about the quilt that laid in her lap. Briskly placing her needle in the pincushion, she set the quilt aside and was on her feet within seconds, her weight leaning on her cane.

"Well, I'm afraid my Ruby may be in some trouble. She hasn't come home, and her *maem* and I are worried. At first, we thought she might be *rutsching* around, but when she wasn't in bed this morning, well..." The bishop paused, his eyes downcast at the floor.

Anna and Beth exchanged glances.

When it was clear that the bishop wasn't going to continue, Anna hobbled a few steps closer and touched the bishop's arm. "Please remember, Bishop Packer, that difficulty is a miracle in its first stage. Everything will be okay - it is *Gotte*'s will. Please, how can we help?" Anna wasn't quite sure what would follow that question. A few months ago, her immediate thoughts would've been that the twins might be asked to help console the bishop's wife, but it crossed her mind that this favor may be bigger than that considering their recent involvement with the investigation into the former county sheriff's murder. The sisters had always been referred to as the "wise women" in the community - would they be asked to help find Ruby?

The sisters knew Ruby, of course. She was the bishop's youngest daughter and possibly the prettiest young teenage girl in the community. She had striking blonde hair and piercing eyes that matched a clear blue sky. The sisters had just recently seen her when they dropped off baked goods to the Packers's home as a thank you gift. She and her friend, Levi Kimes, had been an integral part of saving their lives just a few weeks ago.

Anna straightened up a little without realizing it. She was ready to help in any way necessary. She again looked at Beth who was looking to Anna for a sign that they were on the same wavelength - and with one glance; the sisters knew they were indeed thinking the exact same thing.

Relieved that the sisters didn't ask any questions about how he could've waited so long to investigate, the bishop proceeded, "I know that you two were helpful in communicating with the law on Moses' behalf, and I was wondering if you would join Margaret and myself..."

Beth interrupted the bishop's sentence, "Say no more, Bishop Joseph. We are happy to help in any way that we can."

Anna nodded emphatically.

"*Denki, denki*. Margaret is waiting outside in the buggy now," the bishop said, not wanting to waste any more time than he already had. He had been nervous about approaching the sisters for such a favor and had made sure to ask permission from their husbands, Eli and Noah, beforehand. Eli and Noah had assured the bishop that the women would be excited and more than willing to help. Both husbands trusted and believed that Ruby was fine, and that this would certainly not be as dangerous as the last experience.

The two women grabbed their coats and headed out the door behind the bishop. Beth had returned to driving a buggy just recently and actually looked for an excuse to drive one as often as she could. There weren't many women in the community that drove - mostly men would drive the women where they needed to go, but Beth enjoyed the feeling of independence and freedom it gave her, and her husband trusted her with driving without him.

Beth and Anna told the bishop and his wife they would meet them at the Sheriff's Office shortly and climbed into Beth's buggy.

"Please be careful and take it slow," Anna said.

Beth rolled her eyes. "You always say that, *Schwester*. I'm always careful."

Anna looked at her sister with an all-knowing look and repeated herself, "Just be careful."

With driving lines in hand, Beth cued the horse with a clicking sound. As the horse started to trot, Anna's right hand grabbed onto the side of the buggy, her left hand clutched her cane.

The sisters pulled up to the station a few moments after the Packers had arrived. Their horse was tied to the post, but they had not ascended the steps to the porch just yet.

They stood together waiting for Anna and Beth and a sense of relief washed over their faces when the sisters were in sight.

After securing their horse and exchanging reassuring words with Margaret Packer, the sisters led the way into the Sheriff's Office.

Sheriff Mark Streen rose to his feet as soon as the four Amish citizens entered through the front door. There were three middle-aged women and a gentleman with a long beard and full head of curly brown hair under a straw wide-brimmed hat. The women wore similar plain dresses with aprons. Their hair was pinned neatly underneath their securely fastened *kapps*. Two of the women were identical twins, allowing Sheriff Streen to quickly make the connection that he was meeting the infamous Anna and Beth for the first time. The sheriff was pleasantly surprised to see them and welcomed all of them with a warm smile.

"Hi, folks! Thank you for coming by! I'm the new sheriff in town. Name's Mark Streen. Normally you would get to meet Deputy Chase Brown, too, but he's running a little late this morning." He stretched out his hand to Bishop Packer and Joseph shook his hand, removing his hat with his left hand.

"Welcome to Little Valley, Sheriff. It's good to meet you." The bishop responded.

Anna wanted to interrupt the pleasantries and get right to business, but she worried it would seem disrespectful towards the bishop, so she remained quiet and patient.

The bishop continued, "My name is Joseph Packer. I'm the bishop of the Amish community here in town, and this is my wife, Margaret. These are good friends of ours, Anna Miller and Beth Troyer." He paused briefly before continuing. The sheriff nodded politely at each of the ladies as Bishop Packer introduced them. "We're here today because our daughter, Ruby, is missing. She's thirteen years old, and, well, she didn't come home last night."

"Please have a seat," said the sheriff, quickly collecting the two desk chairs and two visitor chairs and forming a semicircle in front of his desk. He was convinced this office had never seen so many visitors at once, and realizing there were not enough chairs, he promptly leaned on the desk in front of the group and pulled a small black notepad out of his front chest pocket.

"Ok, let's start from the beginning. Your daughter, Ruby, is missing - when was the last time you saw her, sir?" Sheriff Streen asked politely.

"I saw her last at breakfast yesterday morning." He stopped and glanced at Margaret. She grabbed his hand

and gave him an encouraging nod. "To be honest, Sheriff, Ruby and I haven't been getting along very well lately, and she stormed off during breakfast yesterday during a slight disagreement we were having." He looked at the twins seated next to him, afraid of what they were thinking of him with that last bit of information. He wanted badly to be a good father, and he struggled with disciplining his daughters. His first daughter, Esther, had challenged him and accused him of being too strict - and then she had brought him so much shame when she did not return from her *Rumspringa*. And now Ruby was following in her footsteps, repeating the same hurtful actions as her sister. Joseph did not know how he could do things any differently. He was frustrated and had turned to *Gotte* so many times and was still waiting for clarity.

As if he were reading his thoughts, the sheriff responded, "Raising teenagers can be tough, for sure, Bishop Packer - is it okay that I call you that, sir?"

"Yes, that is fine. Thank you," the bishop responded, his voice quiet.

Turning to Margaret, Sheriff Streen asked, "Ma'am, did you see Ruby after breakfast at all?"

Margaret responded without meeting Mark's eyes, her chin quivering as she fought back tears, "No, sir, I am afraid I did not. Ruby has run off like this before. She goes to her friend Grace Schwartz's house. When she does this, I know she is safe and just needs to cool off. I expected her to come home in the middle of the night like she has before, but she wasn't in her room this morning and her bed was still neatly made. I ran to Grace's house myself, but Grace and Mrs. Schwartz said they had not seen her since yesterday afternoon. That is when..." Margaret's voice drifted off and she began to cry, holding a white linen handkerchief to her face. Beth, sitting next to her, reached over and put her arm around her shoulders.

After a quick grateful look at Beth, Joseph continued where Margaret left off. "It's also important to mention, Sheriff, that Ruby is epileptic. She was diagnosed with the seizure disorder just after her fifth birthday. She hasn't had a seizure in several years, but she takes medication every morning, and she doesn't have it with her, as far as I know," he explained. Margaret sobbed quietly and raised her face to look at the sheriff, her wet eyes pleading for an answer.

The Sheriff looked at the notes he had scribbled, taking a quick breath. An epileptic thirteen-year-old girl not returning home for the night was pretty serious, and he knew he couldn't waste any time. He was in a tough spot. This community had been through a lot, and this could either be an opportunity to build more trust among the good people. But if handled poorly, things could rapidly turn the opposite direction.

"Do you have any suspects in mind, Bishop? This can be a hard question, but do you know anyone who would want to hurt Ruby?"

The bishop shook his head emphatically. "We don't personally know anyone that would want to hurt us or our daughter, Sheriff, but someone in our community - a young man named Christopher Yoder - mentioned that he saw a homeless fellow walking on the road near our home the night she didn't come home. We are very concerned that she might be in danger."

"Ah, ok - I'll make sure to meet up with Mr. Yoder and get more details about who and what he saw then," the sheriff responded.

The sheriff stopped writing and looked up. He met Joseph Packer's eyes and with a firm tone, he said, "Bishop, I want to move quickly to get your daughter home safe. I'm going to file a missing persons report and put out what we call an Amber Alert, but first, I'm going to need a photo of Ruby and a description of what she was wearing the last time anyone saw her."

Joseph's heart sank down into his stomach. The Amish community did not take photos, so he could not imagine how he could provide that. And the plain clothing that

Ruby was wearing yesterday could match dozens of girls her age in the community - he wasn't sure that would be much help either.

For the first time, Bishop Packer forgot all of his prideful worries of what people would think of his personal relationship with his daughters, and came face to face with the worst fear of every parent. He looked over at his wife. Margaret's face was turned down, her hands were in her lap and her eyes were closed. Joseph knew she was praying for Ruby's safe return.

Beth reached out and squeezed Anna's hand. They didn't have to say a word or even look at each other to communicate. They both knew they were headed to the Schwartz family farm.

Chapter Eight

C hase was already running late for work. He worried that it might look like he wasn't taking his new job seriously, so he decided to stop at the coffee shop in town to grab a couple of "fancy coffees" for himself and for the Sheriff as a sort of peace offering. He knew he should work harder to make a good impression on the Sheriff, since he had been awarded the deputy position just days before, but it was one of those mornings where everything was going wrong for him. He was hoping to use the excuse of stopping to get coffee in a crowded coffee shop as the reason he was late. He didn't want to lose this job, especially not this soon.

When he pulled up to Coffee World, he fondly remembered how he had first seen Ruby here a few weeks ago. It was a weekend, and he was on lunch break. He had wandered into the only local coffee shop when she immediately caught his eye. She was the most beautiful thing he had ever seen. She was standing in the corner with a girlfriend, waiting on her order to be prepared. When she looked his way, their eyes met, and he held her gaze feeling as if a moment had stopped in time. She smiled at him and her face lit up like an angel. He could see the shine in her brilliant blue eyes from across the room. Her golden blonde hair was pinned neatly into her Amish *kapp*, a style he found very attractive. She was wearing a plain beige Amish dress and apron, but there was nothing else plain about her. She was the most breathtaking girl Chase had ever laid eyes upon, and he was convinced that his world changed instantly.

Chase was standing in the short line to order his coffee when he heard the barista call out the name Ruby. The gorgeous girl reached over to grab her drink, smiled at the barista and thanked her. Chase thought, *even her name is perfect!* Ruby and her friend began walking toward the door. Chase thought she was headed his way, and his stomach filled with butterflies. He felt his face turn red and instinctively, he looked down at the floor.

When he lifted his eyes just a second later, he caught the sight of Ruby and her friend leaving the shop. She had walked right past him. *I'm so stupid!* Chase blamed himself for missing out on the opportunity to speak to someone so incredibly special. He rushed out of the coffee shop, the bell on the door ringing softly as he pushed it open. He was determined to catch up to her and say something - anything. But when he reached the street, there was no sign of her anywhere. He spent the next hour walking around the town's shops and the farmers' market in search of the girl before returning to work.

He was sullen and couldn't get her out of his mind. He even dreamed about Ruby that night when he slept. He was convinced that it was not a mistake that she was set in his path, and he wondered how difficult it would be to convince her to fall in love with him even though he was not of the Amish faith. *We will figure it out together*, he thought.

As if it were destiny, the two crossed paths again the next day. This time, Ruby and a young man, another friend of hers, had come to the station frantic to report that they were witness to a crime. Ruby was terribly shaken, and the boy she was with looked at her longingly as if he wanted to wrap his arms around her to comfort her. Fighting to keep his composure, as well as his career, Chase fought the urge to swoop in and hold her and tell her everything would be alright. He knew it wasn't the right time to do that just yet.

Chase noticed that she kept her distance from her friend, and he wondered if she were trying to show Chase that she wasn't interested in the kid romantically. Before Chase could step in and start a conversation with Ruby, the detective sent her and her friend away and ordered Chase to snap out of it and call for backup.

As much as Chase wanted to run after Ruby again, he knew the timing wasn't right. He didn't want their next meeting to be one associated with witnessing something horrible, so he vowed that he would one day see Ruby again, in a better situation. He made the phone call while he watched her and the boy walk away from the station. He thought he might have seen the boy grab Ruby's hand just as they turned the corner out of sight, but he couldn't be sure.

A few weeks later, when Chase heard that there was an opening for a deputy in the county, at the same exact station, he knew the stars were aligning once again. He couldn't have been happier when he found that he had been selected for the new deputy position. He believed everything in life was all about timing, and it had finally become time to make the next move.

Chase smiled as he jumped out of his car and entered the coffee shop.

Chapter Nine

I t was a Thursday morning, and Moses was busy taking inventory of the different tools in his shop. He took pride in organizing the tools in his shop based on how they should be stored in one's tool box. He recommended that his customers have at least two layers in their toolbox, with the tools that are most often used stored in the top layer. Top layer tools would typically include tools such as a claw hammer, a set of pliers, a flathead screwdriver, a Phillips head screwdriver, an adjustable wrench, and a tape measure. And he had these items displayed in the front of the store since they were his most popular items.

He paused a moment to take a deep breath. He loved being back in his shop. He had come so close to losing it all when he was falsely arrested and, for a brief time, he worried that he would never have this moment again. He loved the way the shop smelled. It was a unique mix of wood and metal. Sarah had commented once, though, on how she didn't care for the way the shop smelled. She made a special candle for him to burn in the shop to replace the scent with "something the customers will like more," as she described it, but the wick remained intact months later. She hardly ever visited the store since the kids were born, but he kept the lighter near the candle just in case she were to ever drop by for a surprise visit. He would be quick about lighting the candle to show his appreciation for the well-meaning gift.

Just as he was returning his focus back to inventory, Moses' attention was turned to the front of the shop as his oldest friend entered wearing the friendly smile that Moses had missed for years.

"Good morning, Moses!" Matthew said, in a melodic voice. "Or should I say *gute mariye*?" He winked and his smile broadened. Matthew was on cloud nine since the bishop and the elders of the community had forgiven him and welcomed him back into the community. He lived in the English world for over a decade, and he missed his dearest friend, Moses. Moses had missed Matthew just as much, and was thrilled to hear he was returning.

"Still getting used to speaking *Dietsch*, eh, Matt?" Moses teased him. "*Wie bischt, bruda?*" Moses asked, reaching out to slap his arm in a friendly manner.

"*Wunderbar*," said Matthew, his accent just as good as the day he left for Rumspringa.

"What brings you to town?" asked Moses, setting his clipboard and pencil down on the counter and turning his full attention to Matthew.

"I was actually sent to purchase a couple new handsaws from you for the Weaver barn project. Seems we have a few more young men training with us this coming weekend, so we could use a couple more tools to put in their hands."

"Ah, *ja*. I will grab those then. Tell me, how are things since you've been back? Anything new happening? Since Rosemary was born, I feel like my life is fuller than ever. I'm missing spending time with friends and hearing the latest news. I haven't had time to help with the community building or anything. I know everyone must think of me as an outcast." Moses ran a hand through his thick hair. He made a mental note to ask Sarah to give him a trim this weekend.

"Things are good. I am staying busy helping whoever needs help around the community. It is an investment in rebuilding relationships with people that had long forgotten me and proving my worth again. I am blessed that I can take some time to do that and live comfortably on my savings for now." Moses felt as if he wasn't quite sure what Matthew had been doing for work in the English world. He wanted to set aside some time to rebuild his relationship with his old friend some time soon.

Matthew continued without missing a beat, "I will say, though, that the elders approached me with something to think about.. I wanted to get your advice, if you have a moment." Matthew trusted Moses more than anyone, and since he was a businessman in Little Valley, he would be the best one to consult on this matter.

Moses was curious. "*Oll recht*," said Moses, nodding.

Matthew explained to Moses how several people in their community had become concerned about the bed-and-breakfast that was being built. It was an Englisher that was building the sort of hotel, which would typically be no worry except that he was fashioning it to look and feel like an Amish home. He was mimicking their farmhouses and serving food that he was labeling as "Amish cuisine." The community wasn't too sure what to think of the fake Amish tourist trap.

On top of that, the Englisher had approached a few of the women at the farmers' market that sold their handmade goods, haggling to buy their crafted items below cost so that he could then turn around and sell them in his establishment. He was promising things that couldn't be trusted - like long term profits. The Englisher didn't seem to want to take no for an answer, and continued to badger the women and to try to sabotage their sales at the market over the past few weeks.

The elders were asking Matthew to step in as a mediator since he had so much experience as an Englisher himself. "My concern, *bruda*, is what if I can't make this guy see the light? What if he doesn't listen to me?"

Moses stroked his beard in thought. "This *Englischer* sounds *deerich*, indeed, and I wonder if he might be dangerous. I worry for your safety, but I also understand the concerns of the community. Since this doesn't really sound like something we could take to the law, though, I see why they are asking you to step in. No matter what, though, mind your step. It sounds like he may be the type with a quick temper. Remember, no matter what he says to you, it is better to give others a piece of your heart than a piece of your mind."

Matthew responded, "Of course, *bruda*. I will be mindful. I will speak with him as two men with the same end goals, and remind him that there is enough tourism to go around for all of us. I am still just so shocked at how busy Little Valley has become since I was last here. The tourists bring with them a good energy, though, and they ultimately bring benefits to all of us. The world is a big place, there's enough room for everyone, even in Little Valley." Matthew smiled.

"*Ja*, it's true. I have faith that we can find a way to get along with the new owner, as well. If he doesn't listen, the next step I would recommend is consulting my mother-in-law and aunt, the twins. They seem to have a way with problem solving and may have more insight. Keep me posted and let me know if I can help with anything, Matt." Moses replied, returning a warm smile beneath his beard.

"I will. *Denki*, Moses. Now, let's get to what I owe you for the tools, and I'll let you get back to counting." Moses wrapped the saws, and with a tip of his hat, Matthew left the shop. He was already on his way to see about meeting with the owner of the bed-and-breakfast.

Chapter Ten

Joseph's face went white when he saw the Sheriff's car stop in front of his house. It had been three days since he had last seen Ruby's face, a carbon copy of his wife's when she was young. It had been three full days since he had last heard her youthful voice and her innocent child-like giggle. His hand shook as he reached for the doorknob and opened the front door. Without a word exchanged, he gestured for Sheriff Streen to enter his quiet home.

He called softly for Margaret to join them in the living room. She rushed in, wiping her hands on her white apron. Her hands had not stopped working since Ruby had vanished. Margaret was not the type of person who could sit still and just wait. Many women from the community had stopped by to offer help and support, but Margaret insisted she needed time to be alone, to work and to pray. Aside from Ruby walking in that front door, these tasks were the only things that could bring her comfort.

The Sheriff removed his cowboy hat, but he remained standing until the older couple took a seat on their couch in front of him. The two sat on the edge of their seats, both literally and figuratively. No words were spoken. The Sheriff thought the parents looked as if they may have aged a bit over the past few days since they first approached him for help to find their teenage daughter. His heart was filled with dread.

Joseph and Margaret sat holding hands. They were afraid to ask the question, but it didn't need to be spoken. It was clear why Sheriff Streen had come to visit.

The Sheriff sat in the large high-backed upholstered chair, situated caddy-cornered to the couch. He also leaned forward, sitting on the edge of his seat, his elbows resting on his knees and his hat dangling by his thumb and index finger. He lifted his face to see Margaret and Joseph pleading with their eyes for the Sheriff to deliver good news.

He cleared his throat before speaking. "Bishop. Mrs. Packer. It pains me to tell you why I'm here today. I'm so sorry, but I do not have good news about your daughter, Ruby." he paused for just a moment, allowing the parents to hold on to each other a little tighter and brace themselves for the words he needed to say next. "Ruby's body was found this morning. I'm afraid she is no longer with us. I am so sorry. I know she was very special, and I want you to know that we will find who is responsible."

A heartbroken scream came bursting out of Margaret's small, fragile body. The sound of her sobs replaced the thick silence that had previously hung in the air of the small room. She collapsed in Joseph's arms, her body shaking, exhausted and grief-stricken. Joseph cried silently, his tears falling onto Margaret's shoulder as they embraced one another. Joseph held his wife close, as if he wanted her to know he would never let her go. Strands of her hair fell out of her *kapp* and around her face, as if her tears were not enough to express her extreme sadness.

The Sheriff cast his eyes back down to the floor out of respect. He continued to sit quietly, sharing the solemn moment with the Packers for a while longer. He had never carried this sort of burden in all the years that he was on the police force, and he was running strictly on instinct, waiting silently for them to make the next move. He figured the bereaved parents would either ask him to leave or ask for more information, but he was going to let them dictate which of those actions he took and comply in the best way that he could.

When Joseph could speak again, he uttered one word just barely above a whisper, "Where?" He wasn't prepared to ask for any more details just yet - not in front of his wife. He wanted to see his daughter, and he knew his wife would want that, too. He would have more questions, but not until after he saw that Margaret, and Ruby, were taken care of.

"She was found in the woods just about a mile away, Bishop." The Sheriff spoke softly and carefully, hoping to lessen the heartache. "Tall trees and beautiful wildflowers surrounded her. She laid peacefully next to a small stream until Levi Kimes found her. I understand he was a close friend of Ruby's."

The bishop nodded. His tears suddenly stopped falling as if there were none left and a numbness seemed to take over his entire body. Still holding onto Margaret, his mind began spinning. *She was in town? Surrounded by flowers? Left in the woods to die?* Nothing was making any sense.

Among many, the bishop's emotions were those of shock, regret and guilt. *This can't be real,* he thought.

Margaret lifted her head and looked directly at the Sheriff. Her eyes were red and swollen, her face was tear-stained and her expression was one of confusion, sadness, and fear all together in one. Her expression at that moment would leave an impression on Sheriff Streen's memory for a lifetime. Her mouth opened as if she wanted to speak, but there was no sound. Joseph interjected and asked the question that both parents wanted to know: "When can we see her?"

Chapter Eleven

Word spreads fast among Little Valley, especially something so paralyzing as this. The sisters took charge of planning the arrangements.

"Grace's father has offered to make the coffin," said Anna. "And Moses will make the gravestone."

"How can you just jump right into planning the ceremony, *schwester*, as if this wasn't a murder? We have to help find the killer! He could still be among us!" Beth exclaimed, pulling on her sister's arm to get her attention.

"*Ja*, Beth, I know. But, need I remind you that we are not detectives? What do you think? Just because we got involved with freeing Moses does not mean that we are trained police officers, now does it? My knee isn't even all the way healed from our last excursion, and to be honest with you, I'm worried about the fact that there have been such terrible crimes. And in such a short time. I'm starting to wonder if Little Valley is where we should stay." Anna's words poured out like water out of a broken faucet.

"What are you saying, Anna? Do you want to leave Little Valley? How could you say that? All of our family is here! We have lived here all of our lives and have many years left." Beth shook her head in disbelief.

Anna held Beth's hand and responded with a persuasive tone, "Beth, just think. Over the past few months, our lives have been impacted by robberies and murder. And it's not just that. Little Valley is changing. Tourism is growing, and it's not all good. We have someone in town that is building a bed-and-breakfast that mimics our lifestyle for profit, and we have drifters now!"

Beth interrupted, "We have heard of only one drifter, Anna."

Anna continued persistently, "but what if he did this to Ruby? We can't be sure that we are still safe here."

Beth took a deep breath and reached up to gently turn Anna's face back to hers. "That is why we have to get involved, Anna. We can investigate and find out what happened to poor Ruby and set our minds at ease. If it's the drifter, he will be arrested and the new sheriff will put new laws into effect to keep any other danger out of Little Valley."

Anna looked long and hard at Beth before shaking her head slowly. "You are naive, *schwester*." She paused. Anna didn't want to rule out moving away. She had privately been discussing it with Eli. She knew how Beth panicked when she was faced with change, and then there were their children. Beth was right about leaving their family behind, but Anna hoped they would all be on board. And she needed Beth to help research possible areas to relocate that were safer but close enough to easily return to visit if they wanted.

"I am going to remind you, Anna, of our mother's favorite proverb: Regrets over yesterday and the fear of tomorrow are twin thieves that rob us of the moment." Beth said as if that was the end to the conversation.

Anna rolled her eyes, "Sister, I think you're taking that too literally," she continued, "but I promise that I will put these thoughts on the shelf for now - at least until after Ruby's funeral service. Promise me, Beth, that this will be our secret until we decide together what is best."

Beth hated secrets, but she promised her sister that she wouldn't tell anyone. She vowed to herself that she would try very hard to change her sister's mind about Little Valley. It was their home, and Beth wanted to stay there forever.

Beth and Anna had just turned their attention back to Ruby's celebration of life when Noah walked in with Sheriff Streen in tow.

"Beth and Anna, look who I found in the front." Sheriff Streen's cowboy hat was in hand and he nodded at the sisters, his face unable to hide the stress and worry that he carried.

"*Hallo*, Sheriff," Anna and Beth said in unison.

"What can we do for you?" Anna took the lead.

Noah responded before the sheriff had a chance to mutter a word, "He is here to ask you two a few questions about Ruby's disappearance, and, you know..."

The sheriff nodded. "If you two have a minute," he asked, politely.

The twins nodded in agreement. Anna could feel Beth's excitement stirring. Noah bid farewell and headed out the kitchen backdoor, anxious to get back to work.

"Can I offer you some tea?" Anna asked the sheriff. "The kettle is still warm."

"No, thank you, ma'am," the sheriff looked as if he was distracted, fidgeting with his hat and his eyes shifting. "I won't be long. I just thought I should come by to check on you, first of all. Since you were with the Packers at my office the other day, I am assuming y'all knew Ruby pretty well. How are you doing?"

"*Gotte* is there to give us strength for every hill we have to climb. We believe that Ruby was called to a living hope of salvation with *Gotte*. We were just planning her celebration of life." Beth responded as Anna nodded in agreement.

The sheriff wasn't sure if he should be surprised by their lack of grief showing or if that was just 'the Amish way,' for everyone except those closest to the victim, of course. He nodded and waited for a brief moment before continuing.

"Good, good," he said, hoping that agreement was the right response and wanting to get to business. "I won't deny that the reason I'm here is because the two of you have quite the reputation among the local law folk for your recent involvement in a murder case. It wasn't even that long ago, was it?

Anna noticed Beth's knee started moving slightly in a steady rhythm. She knew Beth was about to burst with anticipation, and she herself started to feel a sense of unease. She knew they were lucky to walk away safely from the last adventure and she had no interest in risking her and her sister's lives again. She wasn't sure why, but a kidnapping and a murder of someone in their own community felt much more dangerous than finding an Englisher dead in

Moses' toolshed behind his shop. She also knew that she cared deeply for the bishop and Margaret, and she couldn't imagine what it must be like to not know who did this to their daughter.

The sheriff continued speaking during Anna's train of thought. "I am hoping that you two might be able to shed some light on the case." The sheriff noticed the sisters looking at each other. Neither responded, so he continued, "anything you can contribute at all..."

Snapping out of her swirling thoughts, Anna tightened her *kapp*, stood up leaning on her cane, and said, "Sheriff, we will help you find who did this."

The sheriff looked confused. "Um, wait. That's not ..." he stuttered.

Beth was on her feet, too, and with a louder voice than the sheriff and Anna expected, she chimed in, "Yes, thank you, Sheriff, for reaching out to us. We will see what we can find out and help get to the bottom of this."

The sheriff was flabbergasted and not sure if he should encourage this or not. On the one hand, he couldn't expect these older women to make much of a dent in the investigation, but on the other hand, he had hit a brick wall with the drifter being cleared with a solid alibi and lack of motive.

Beth reached out her hand with an invite for a handshake from the sheriff. Anna chuckled at her sister as she ushered Sheriff Streen out the door.

Finally gathering himself, the sheriff stopped on the porch just outside the front door and said, "Wait. I need you to know that I didn't actually come here to enlist you two as my deputies. I only wanted to ask if you knew anything. I have Deputy Brown for help. I do *not* want you to get hurt - I hope you are hearing that loud and clear. I don't mind you asking questions from the locals since so many people know and trust you around here, but don't go investigating and doing detective work without my knowing about it. Do you promise?"

Anna was actually relieved to hear the sheriff say those words, but Beth had already turned into the house to collect her coat. All thoughts of planning the funeral service were replaced by finding Ruby's killer.

To Beth, that also meant there would be an end to secrets and a guaranteed lifetime of happiness in Little Valley for her and her family.

Chapter Twelve

Levi's parents were worried about him. They knew that he and Ruby Packer were friends, and that finding her body in the woods was devastating. But they weren't sure if or when he would return to the normal happy kid that they had raised.

Levi went through the motions each minute of every day, but he was overcome with guilt. He couldn't stop picturing Ruby's face, once flawless and full of joy, and then, still, pale, and lifeless. His heart ached like he had never experienced before, and at times he would have trouble breathing. There were no tears to bring relief. There was no sleep for escape. Their secret died with Ruby - and he planned to keep it with him forever, like a locked chest of treasure.

The sheriff appeared in the large open doorway of the barn. Levi tried to keep his breathing steady and his face emotionless. He watched as the sheriff and his father had a conversation, but the tone was too low to make out what they were saying. Both men turned to look at Levi and time slowed down, as if suspended. Levi's father gestured for him and somehow Levi felt his body start to move, slowly, one careful step at a time, his gaze never leaving his father's face.

His father said something about Levi needing to go with the sheriff to the office to answer questions, and all Levi could do was nod. His voice had stopped working - Levi struggled to mumble even the smallest word. He wanted to grab hold of his *dat* and tell him everything. He wanted to cry out for help and let the truth roll off his tongue, but something was keeping him from doing any of that.

For the first time in his life, Levi sat in an English car - the sheriff's car - and he wasn't sure he would even remember it at all. He turned to look out the back window. He saw his father briskly jumping into the family's buggy, securing his hat and roughly whipping the driving lines, motioning the strong horse to move quickly. His mother stood on the threshold of the house, she had her apron crinkled in her hands as if it were a handkerchief. Levi regretted the cloud of concern that hovered over her face. He knew he was the cause of all of this, and he wished more than anything that he could just turn back time.

They arrived at the sheriff's office in what felt like record time to Levi. Sheriff Streen stepped out of the car and opened Levi's door for him, gesturing him to exit the car and come inside. Levi followed along as if he were a tamed horse.

Walking into the front office, Levi's head hung low. Deputy Chase Brown was sitting straight in the antique desk chair behind the smaller desk. His face was directed at Levi, his expression was a mixture of contempt, anger, and disgust - but to his disappointment, Levi didn't even notice he was in the room. Chase noticed Levi's glazed look and wondered if he even knew where he was at.

Sheriff Streen had noticed Levi's face, as well. He needed to ask Levi some important questions considering he was Ruby's friend and he was the one who found her dead, but he was afraid that the kid might need counseling instead. In an attempt to put Levi at ease, he led him into the kitchen area and shut the heavy door leading to the jail cell. He showed Levi where the bathroom was located and he offered him a bottle of water. Levi seemed to barely comprehend the question and shook his head no before looking back towards the ground.

The sheriff wished Levi's father would arrive so they could get on with the questions, and he was starting to regret asking him to come into the office at all. He was hoping that it would have the opposite effect on him and lead to some clues, but he was starting to wonder if Levi was even capable of answering questions at all in the state he was in. And, he didn't want to traumatize the kid anymore than he clearly already had been.

Levi's father finally walked through the front door of the Sheriff's Office just as Levi sat in one of the visitor chairs placed directly in front of the sheriff's desk.

"Ok, thank you for coming out this way, Mr. Mast. I'm not sure Levi is feeling too well, so I'll try to make this quick." The sheriff picked up a pen and set his reading glasses on his nose. "I just need to ask your son what he remembers about the day that he found Ruby in the woods."

Mr. Mast looked at Levi who stared straight ahead with a blank stare, mouth slightly open. "Can you tell the sheriff what you remember, son?" he asked, after putting his arm around his son's shoulders. He could tell Levi was scared and he wished he could erase all of this.

"I don't know..." Levi's voice was quiet and trailed off as if lost in the wind.

After a pause, the sheriff then asked another question, "Can you tell me what you were doing out there that day, Levi? It was early in the morning, wasn't it?"

Levi sucked in air and closed his mouth tight. He shook his head and looked at his father. Mr. Mast felt a tug at his heart. He pictured Levi as a young five-year-old boy. He instantly remembered the day when Levi had climbed the ladder to the roof of the barn. Once on top of the roof, he became so scared of falling that he couldn't find the courage to step back down the ladder. Levi's father had to climb up the ladder and help him find his footing on every step of the way down. And he was willing to help him find his footing again now, faced with the memories of finding someone - a friend of his even - dead on the ground in the woods. He didn't know why he was out there, either, and had wanted to ask Levi that question himself, but he trusted there must have been a good reason.

Mr. Mast turned his attention back to the sheriff. "My apologies, sir, but I think I need to take my son home. I can reach out once he is feeling better or if he remembers anything that might be helpful."

The sheriff had no reason to keep Levi - he wasn't a suspect, and he was a minor - so, he nodded in agreement. He rose to his feet, reached out to shake Mr. Mast's hand, apologized for taking his time and thanked him again for coming out. He watched as the father and son pair left the office and walked to the window to watch as they climbed into their buggy, heading back to their home.

He let out a sigh. He was at a dead end. He was secretly hoping the twin sisters would find something - maybe the boy would feel more comfortable talking to them.

As the sheriff went to take his seat, Deputy Brown spoke up for the first time since Levi had set foot in the office and said, "If you ask me, that boy is as guilty as a bear with his paw in a beehive."

Chapter Thirteen

The twin sisters entered the diner and chose seats at the counter. The diner was empty - lunch was still a few hours away. Anna and Beth wanted to chat with Jessica McLean, the owner, and see if she had heard anything out of the ordinary from the Englishers about Ruby's disappearance and murder. With their booth at the farmers market scheduled for the next day and Ruby's funeral on Sunday, and now their investigation underway, their lives had become very busy. They spent the morning baking their mother's favorite apple butter cakelets, preparing the caramel sauce separately. Plus, at the request of Anna's daughter, Sarah, they had also made a couple batches of the butterscotch cinnamon rolls that they had perfected together over the years, setting aside some for the sale. The sisters also wanted to drop some off as a thank you gift for Mr. Hatfield for the beautiful flowers he brought for Moses' party. And they had made just enough to bring to Jessica to add to her case of baked goods that she offered her customers.

After all the baked goods were packed up and the kitchen was clean again, the sisters were off on their mission to get to the bottom of who was behind the latest crime.

Anna and Beth could hear the clatter of porcelain plates and pots and pans behind the swinging doors leading to the kitchen area of the diner. Jessica was busy cleaning up from breakfast and preparing for the lunch crowd. The doors pushed open and Jessica appeared in front of the twins. Her face lit up with a warm smile when she saw the two middle-aged women sitting at the counter. She was holding a wet dingy rag and a bottle of cleaner and her wavy red hair flowed down her back, the sides tied back away from her face. A few curly strands of hair had fallen near her temples complimenting her fair skin and blue eyes. Light freckles looked as if they were sprinkled like fairy dust on the bridge of her nose and fullness of her cheeks. She was a very attractive woman, young and sweet. Although the twins had visited with Jessica on several occasions, Anna realized now that she really didn't know much about her personal life. She made a mental note to make an effort to get to know her better after things settled down. She was reminded of her conversation with Beth the day before about considering moving out of Little Valley and she pushed away the sadness that followed her thoughts.

"Oh my gosh, hi ladies! I am so glad to see you! How long were you sitting here? I'm so sorry to keep you waiting!" Jessica spoke quickly, her voice friendly and excited. Before waiting for Anna and Beth to respond, she spotted the white box and exclaimed, "Oh! Please tell me that is some of your delicious baked goods that you have brought for me!" She set the cleaning supplies down and stood with one hand on her hip.

Beth was the first to answer. She felt comfortable around her, which said a lot about Jessica since Beth often felt uneasy around people, especially those outside of the community. "We made butterscotch cinnamon rolls. We just know you'll love them. We finally perfected the recipe and they sell out pretty quickly at the market when we have them on the table."

Jessica closed her eyes briefly and brought her hand to her stomach as if she was imagining just how delicious the rolls tasted, "Oh, wow, I can't wait to try those! I'm not even sure I'm going to share them with my customers - I may just keep them all to myself!" She chuckled. And then, as if remembering her manners, she said, "Thank you both so much. That is very sweet that you thought of me. What can I get for you? Are you hungry for brunch? Tea? Coffee?"

Anna responded with a wave of the hand, "Oh, I'm not hungry. I'll just take a cup of coffee if you have some already freshly made. No sugar or cream, please." She looked to Beth.

"I'll take the same, please, Jessica," Beth said. There were only a very few things that the sisters ever did differently - so few that they could be counted on one hand. They had the same favorite food: chicken and dressing. Blackberries were their favorite fruit, and they both favored the color light blue. The twins cooked and baked the exact same way - so much so that their own husbands couldn't tell their breads apart - and the same applied to their sewing and cleaning. There was a slight difference in how they pinned their hair, what books they chose at the library, and Beth liked to drive a buggy where Anna preferred to ride, but that was about it.

Jessica poured hot coffee into three separate mugs and invited the women to join her in the large corner booth. "This is actually perfect timing for a break," she said, settling in across from Anna and Beth. "I think I could probably guess why the two of you are here today, although it's always great to see you."

Anna spoke, "Thank you - we feel the same, but, yes, we should probably get straight to the point so you can get ready for your lunch customers. Forgive me if I am being too direct, but have you heard or seen anything strange - you know, about sweet little Ruby Packer's vanishing and death? I'm afraid the sheriff doesn't have much of a lead, and our whole community is just in shock.. and scared."

"If we can help solve the murder then we're sure to set a lot of minds at ease," Beth interjected. "The Packers, as you can imagine, are just so shocked that someone would want to hurt their youngest daughter."

Jessica nodded, "Oh, I cannot imagine what they must be going through. It is just terrible." She paused for a moment to take a sip of the hot coffee. "I've been thinking about it," she said, leaning in towards the sisters. She lowered her voice instinctively despite the empty room. "I'm not sure if y'all know that the new deputy was rejected by Ruby right before she went missing."

The sisters shook their heads, "No, what do you mean?" Anna asked, her curiosity peaked.

Jessica continued, her words flowing out quickly as if she was going to burst if she didn't tell someone. "Well, there were a few people sitting at the counter, so I know I'm not the only one who saw it, and honestly, I kinda feel bad for the guy. But, yeah, Ruby was here with her best girlfriend - I think her name is Grace. Those two are such sweet girls, well..." She caught herself speaking in the present tense and decided not to correct herself. "They were sitting here sharing a piece of cake near the end of the busy lunch hour last weekend. The deputy had walked in and walked right up to them, like he came in specifically to see them - not to eat. He didn't look around for a place to sit or anything. He stuck out his hand for a handshake - to Ruby, understand. He was pretty much ignoring Grace. And he introduced himself. I think he said his name was Jason, but I'm not sure. Then he said that he was the new deputy. Ruby looked a little confused, probably wondering why this guy, a few years older than her, was bent on talking to her exactly. She definitely looked like this was the first time she was seeing this guy." Jessica took another sip before continuing. The sisters were hanging on her every word, nodding quietly here and there.

"So, anyway, he said he had seen her at the coffee shop before and he wanted to tell her that he thought she was the most beautiful girl he had ever seen. Just like that! He said it just like that!" Jessica exclaimed, shaking her head as if she still just couldn't believe it. "I was thinking, is this guy flirting with Ruby? He had at least three or four years on her. I mean, yeah, she's strikingly pretty, but she's so young!"

"Well, Ruby turned all shades of pink and looked even more uncomfortable, I'll tell ya. I don't even think she responded to that - and I'm not sure he really needed a response to it, now that I think about it. He continued on and said he wanted to take her out on a date. Just like that. He didn't *ask* her out on a date, understand me. He said the words, 'I wanna take you on a date.' Well, that's when Ruby looked over at me. I had made my way over to her by now, sensing that she might need some backup. And I asked her if everything was alright. Instead of answering me, she looked up at the deputy and responded simply, 'No thank you. I am not dating yet.' and that was that. That girl was so confident. I was proud of her." Jessica stopped talking, waiting for a reaction from the women sitting across from her.

Beth was intrigued, "Well, what happened next? How did the young man react when Ruby told him that?"

Jessica shrugged, "I'm not really clear where it went from there. At that exact moment, Samuel Graber came in making a scene, and I was pulled away to deal with that again. But, when I turned back, they had all left. There was a tip on the counter with the empty plate. I can only assume that the boy took the hint and bowed out - and that Ruby and Grace left for home. That was the last time I saw her. I'm so sad about that. I really liked her." Jessica's voice had slowed, and her eyes misted over. "It just breaks my heart that someone did something so terrible to her."

Beth and Anna nodded in agreement. "Yes, it's true, but in our faith, we believe that creation and destruction are the two ends of the same moment. Ruby has found salvation with the Lord, and although she will be missed, we trust that *Gotte* has a perfect plan," Anna explained.

Beth picked up right where Anna left off and said, "Jessica, you said that Samuel came in making a ruckus. What was that about?"

Jessica rolled her eyes. "It's always something with Samuel," she said. "He was pretty angry. I guess he had just found out that the sheriff shut down gaming in his bar, for good." She hesitated and then with her eyebrows pushed together, she looked back and forth slowly from sister to sister and said, "It wouldn't be right for me to not mention that Samuel has been going around outwardly threatening your community. I mean, y'all probably already know that, but in case you don't, please be careful, he is a volatile person, and it sounds like he blames y'all's community for the whole gaming shutdown and he intends to make someone pay for it."

Anna looked surprised, "What do you mean? What does he intend to do?"

Jessica relaxed her shoulders and leaned back in the seat, "I'm not sure he'll do anything, to be honest. I personally think he's all talk. He really used to be a nice guy. It's just that his drinking has gotten so much worse, and I think he is gettin' caught up with the wrong crowd. I seen him hanging out with that new Englisher, Hank somebody. You know, he's the one that is building that bed-and-breakfast on the west side of town. Those two seem like they're in cahoots about something, huddling together in this here booth, talking with hushed tones. I think they're up to no good, but they're mostly pretty harmless like two young boys acting like fools."

"I see," said Anna. "Well, I'll be sure to pass the word to the community, if not just for safety. Thank you for letting us know."

"Yes, thank you for everything, Jessica," said Beth, "but we should probably run. We have to meet with Mrs. Packer and finalize Sunday's funeral arrangements."

"Oh, please let me know if I can do anything at all to help," Jessica said, cleaning supplies in hand again.

"You've been a wonderful help today," Anna assured her. Jessica was relieved to hear it. She often wondered if she said too much and worried that she gave the wrong information or impression of something, but she would admit that it felt good to tell someone all of this. She also wondered why the new sheriff hadn't come to ask her anything yet. She looked forward to getting to know him better. She hoped he was a better guy than the previous sheriff in Little Valley.

The twins thanked Jessica again and headed on their way. Once they sat in the buggy, Beth picked up the driving lines, but paused and looked at Anna. "We just got so much information, *schwester*. It almost looks like we could have two, possibly three potential suspects! The deputy, that terrible man, Samuel - and Hank Davis, too."

Anna nodded, "*Ja*, I know. I was thinking the same thing, *schwester*. One thing is for sure, there are a lot of secrets in Little Valley. But, I am confident that we are much closer to the truth than we were this morning."

Beth agreed. "Let's head to see Mrs. Packer. We are later than expected," she said just before she signaled for the horse to trot forward.

Inside the diner, Jessica snuck her first taste of the delicious butterscotch cinnamon rolls. *There's no way I'm sharing these*, she said to herself, as she placed the plain bakery box behind the counter to take home with her after closing.

Chapter Fourteen

Margaret Packer stood in her kitchen, one hand caught in midair holding a half peeled hard-boiled egg. Her other hand was resting on the counter. Her eyes were fixed on the empty rope swing in the backyard. The swing hung from a branch in an old oak tree, and she watched it as it swayed softly in the gentle breeze. *Ruby is with Gotte now*, she recited in her mind again. The whole thing seemed so hard to believe, and she found comfort in saying those 5 words to herself throughout the day. She set the egg down and turned to take a sip from the hot steaming cup of meadow tea sitting on the table behind her.

She glanced out the front window, checking to see if Anna and Beth had arrived yet. Joseph had left about an hour before to visit Jacob Schwartz. Grace Schwartz was Ruby's best friend and her father, Jacob, had built the coffin for Ruby's funeral tomorrow. He and Joseph planned to transport the coffin into town to the funeral home so that they could have everything ready for tonight's viewing and tomorrow's ceremony. Anna and Beth were going to visit with Margaret and make sure all the other accommodations for the event were in place. Margaret was preparing a light lunch for the women to share.

There was no sign of Anna and Beth's buggy yet, so Margaret turned back to finish preparing the egg salad. Just as she was finishing setting the table, she spotted their buggy. It surprised her to see Beth as the driver, but she had heard that she had taken to driving her and her sister everywhere. She opened the front door and welcomed each of the women with a hug.

"*Denki* for coming," said Margaret as she gestured to take their coats.

"Of course, Margaret. *Wie bischt?*" Anna asked with compassion in her eyes. Margaret appreciated the effort but had already grown tired of the special treatment she was receiving. She never expected for parenting to be such a challenge and full of heartache. First, her daughter Esther had broken her heart by choosing to leave the faith and now, someone had taken her beautiful Ruby away. Margaret had chosen her name based on the scriptures, specifically Proverb 3:15, "She is more precious than rubies; nothing you desire can compare with her." *Ruby was indeed precious*, Margaret fought back tears as she grappled with her grief. *Ruby is with Gotte now.*

Clearing her throat, Margaret avoided Anna's question and invited the girls to sit down and eat with her. "Would either of you like meadow tea with your lunch? I have made my mother's famous egg salad and we have bread and butter to share."

Beth responded, "Oh, you shouldn't have, but that sounds delicious! I love your mother's egg salad recipe - it's the one with green olives and pimento, right? Your recipe has inspired mine for many years. It's my husband, Noah's, favorite."

"*Ja*, it is delicious, Margaret, and I would say that Beth's is pretty close," Anna said lightheartedly as the women took their seat. "I'll just have water, I think, though. *Denki.*"

"Me too, Margaret. Water is fine for me, as well." Beth chimed in. "We just had coffee at the diner with Jessica.

We went to ask..." Anna kicked Beth under the table, and Beth stuttered, "I mean, we went to bring her some of our baked goods. For her customers, I mean." Beth recovered, realizing that she almost put her foot in her mouth telling Margaret the real reason for their visit with Jessica.

"Ah, how is business for Jessica, then? I haven't seen her in a while, it seems." Margaret asked, filling the three glasses in front of her with water from the steel pitcher.

"She seems well. She sends offerings of help if you need anything at all," Anna spoke carefully, still unsure if Margaret was ready to discuss Ruby and wanting to be respectful.

"That's very kind. Joseph and I have been showered with kindness the past couple days." Margaret responded, her words trailing off as she pushed the dish of egg salad toward the women.

The women helped themselves and since the door to the conversation had been opened, Anna continued, "Do you need any help, Margaret? Anything at all? I mean, Beth and I are helping to organize tomorrow's ceremony, but is there anything else we can do for you?"

Margaret sat staring at the cup of tea placed next to her glass of water, her plate was empty. She needed to talk to someone about what she found in Ruby's room, and she trusted Beth and Anna. "Yes," she finally spoke. "I do need something. I need to share a secret that I am holding, and I know I can trust the two of you to know what to do with it." She looked up and her eyes met Anna's. If one's eyes are the window to their soul, Anna thought, then she was sure that Margaret's soul was troubled, overwhelmed, and most importantly, she was lost. She reached out to take her hand into hers.

"Certainly we can help," Anna said with strength in her voice. "First, let us pray together." Beth closed the circle by holding Anna's and Margaret's free hands, and the women bowed their heads. "O Lord, we thank you for this nourishing food we are about to eat as well as for the family that we sit in company with. Almighty *Gotte* and Heavenly Father, you who know and recognize everyone's heart, we ask you to help and guide us to make the right decisions during this time of distress. Teach us to act according to your will, for you are our God." Beth recited the prayer quietly.

After a brief pause, the women said "Amen" in unison.

"*Denki*, Beth, that was beautiful," Margaret said, taking a sip of her tea. "I had a late breakfast, so I think I'll just munch on a piece of bread, but please enjoy." She motioned to the women to begin eating despite her empty plate.

After compliments for the tasty lunch were given and received, Anna speaks up, "What is this secret you are carrying on your shoulders, Margaret? We want to help in any way we can."

Margaret straightened up in her seat, reminded that she had mentioned it a moment before. "Oh yes," she said. "Let me go grab it and I'll be right back." She left the room quickly and returned just seconds later with a school notebook in hand. She placed the notebook in front of the sisters. "I found Ruby's diary last night."

Beth let out a short gasp. "*Ach du lieva*," she muttered.

Margaret's hand laid on top of the diary. She continued, "You must understand that I haven't shared this with Joseph yet. There are some things in here that may hurt him deeply, and I want to avoid that."

"Ruby is a good girl, but she is very confused about why her older sister left the faith. She misses Esther - the two girls were close - and she blames her father for most of it." Anna noticed how Margaret spoke of Ruby in the present tense, and for a moment, she wondered if Margaret could heal from this. Her life would look very different now, and Anna couldn't imagine what that must feel like.

"But, there is something near the end - in the more recent entries - that is really shocking. I guess Ruby and Levi Mast were sort of secretly dating. Ruby mentions a few times that Levi had more serious feelings than she did, and they were meeting in secret. She wrote that no one else knew about it except for Grace - Grace Schwartz, her best friend. I know what you're thinking - it's embarrassing and a big part of why I haven't told anyone yet, especially Joseph. Ruby was only thirteen." Margaret caught herself from using present tense that time before continuing, "She shouldn't have been breaking the rules."

She let out a heavy sigh, removed her hand from the diary and slumped back in her chair, feeling a mixture of emotions, but relieved to have finally shared what she had found. It had been so hard to keep this secret from Joseph even for this short of time. But, he loved Ruby so much and he would be shocked to know of her breaking the rules of their faith like this.

Beth wanted to grab the book and devour it like a lion who hasn't eaten in weeks, but more importantly, she wanted to be respectful. "May we read it?" Beth asked gingerly.

"*Ja*, you may." Margaret nodded, thanking her for asking.

The sisters pushed their lunches aside and opened the notebook carefully. Ruby's handwriting was straight and neat. She started each page with "Dear Diary" on the top left and the date on the top right. Margaret was right, there were quite a few pages concerning disagreements with her father, followed by detailed accounts of her encounters with Levi.

What Margaret didn't mention, however, was the several entries right alongside the recent entries of her escapades with Levi where Ruby mentioned that she felt as if she was being watched, or followed. Ruby couldn't seem to shake the uneasy feeling she got during these episodes, which happened mostly in the evenings or early mornings, she had recorded. Ruby also mentioned that her mother disregarded it, describing Ruby's fear as the result of Ruby's "overactive imagination." Ruby wrote that she desperately wanted her mother to believe her - that her fears felt very real.

Margaret sat patiently across the table from the sisters waiting for them to finish reading. As soon as the book closed, she spoke, "Well, do you think Levi could have..." she didn't want to say the words out loud, but she knew she had to... "hurt Ruby? Do you think he could have hurt her? I don't know him very well, and he is so young. But I don't know what to do."

The sisters were stunned. This diary may very well be an important piece of the puzzle.

Beth spoke, "We couldn't say for sure, Margaret. I think we are both shocked about Ruby and Levi's secret, but I can't imagine young Levi...."

"But, I do think it's important to tell the sheriff about this, Margaret. We can impress on the sheriff how important it is to keep the details secret for as long as we can, but if it could help find who did this, well, then, that is what is best for the community overall." Anna interjected. "Everyone knows that Ruby loved her father, Margaret, and he will forgive her words when they reach his ears."

Margaret nodded and then replied meekly, "If you think it could help the investigation..."

"With your permission then, we will hand over the diary with care to the sheriff. We have met him and he seems kind and respectful - he's not like Sheriff McCall. We can trust him." Anna responded, again, holding Margaret's hand in her own.

"Now, let's get busy setting up for tonight's viewing," Beth said, "..if you're ready, Margaret?"

"*Ja*, I am ready," Margaret said out loud, rising from her seat. In her mind, she recited those five words: *Ruby is with Gotte now.*

Chapter Fifteen

Ruby's funeral was indeed a celebration of life, full of beautifully sung hymns and solemn prayer and silence. Amish communities from miles away traveled to attend and show the Packers comfort. Margaret and Joseph's oldest daughter, Esther, attended the funeral as well. She sat in the front, in a modest English black dress, hair pinned up with a black lace covering the top and back of her head. She held her mother's hand throughout the service and then hugged her tightly goodbye directly after the burial ceremony. She chose not to exchange words or hugs with her father, and it appeared as if he expected nothing else.

The community of Little Valley gathered together for a celebratory meal after the burial proceedings. Anna and Beth had prepared food for the masses and as with most gatherings in their community, the men tended to gather outside, in the barn or the yard. The women stayed inside and visited among each other, providing comfort to those closest to Ruby and telling beautiful stories about her life.

"Can I please have a moment to speak with you?" Grace tugged on Anna's arm, touching Beth's arm, as well. She couldn't remember if she had ever spoken directly to the older twin sisters before now, and she was a bit nervous. She had heard so much about how Mrs. Miller and Mrs. Troyer had freed Moses and she knew they were known as the wise women in the community. And it was for both of these reasons that she needed desperately to speak with them.

Anna and Beth looked at each other. They recognized the young girl right away as Jacob's daughter and Ruby's best friend, but Anna wondered if they should step away. Margaret was just a few steps away, seated on a comfortable chair, her own mother on one side and her cousin on the other. They were drinking tea and having quiet conversation. Anna decided they could step away for just a few moments, and Beth took no convincing to do so.

Grace felt a sense of relief when the two women agreed to join her outside to talk privately. She followed Anna and Beth out the side door and down the wooden porch steps. There were two sturdy benches there set next to each other, facing out to the open field. There were many sunsets that the Packer family had watched from these seats over the years, and Grace remembered sitting on them with Ruby a time or two, as well. The women sat next to each other and Grace sat on the other, turned toward them slightly.

Grace closed her eyes and took in a calming breath. Today was difficult for her, despite the faith that Ruby was with the Lord. She missed her best friend terribly and couldn't imagine a life without her in it. She blinked back tears and faced the sisters. She noticed how much they looked alike and definitely couldn't say which was which if she were asked.

"*Denki* for talking with me," she said, her voice trembling.

"Of course, Grace," Anna answered, waiting for Grace to continue.

"Ruby and I were best friends," she said quietly. She again tried to blink back tears, but one escaped and slowly trickled down her cheek. "We grew up together, and we told each other everything."

Beth leaned forward and touched her shoulder, "*Ja*, we know this is hard. Take your time. Let us know how we can help you."

Grace took another deep breath and exhaled slowly. "*Denki*. The thing is that Ruby told me something in confidence and I promised not to tell another soul. And I haven't. I haven't told anyone at all. But I think Ruby would want me to tell someone now that she's... gone." Grace looked down at the grass in front of her. She wasn't sure if this was the right thing to do, and she was scared. She didn't want Ruby's father to be angry with her, but she was conflicted. She knew they had not found who killed her best friend and Ruby's secrets might bring justice to that terrible person.

She looked back at the twins, her eyes wet and dull, and tried to speak but her nerves were causing her to struggle. Now that she had the women's attention, she wasn't sure where to begin. Just when she started to doubt her decision to say anything at all, Anna spoke.

"Grace, we know about Levi," she said in a kind voice that she hoped would bring comfort to the young girl.

Grace's face and neck flushed a slight tinge of red and her eyes widened. "You do?" she asked in surprise.

Beth answered, "*Ja*, we know they were in love and were meeting secretly."

"Well, I don't know if you could say they were in love exactly. Levi may have said they were, but Ruby wasn't sure. She was just, well, she liked Levi, but she told me she wasn't in love with him. They weren't *schmunzla* or anything like that. Ruby said they would just talk when they met in the woods. She thought he was very nice, and I think that she liked the attention he gave her mostly."

When Grace took a pause, Beth asked, "Did you say they met in the woods?"

Grace nodded, "*Ja*, they had a secret spot where they would meet. Ruby loved it there, but she would complain that Levi was usually late." Still turned toward the twins, her right foot hanging off the bench didn't quite touch the ground. Her leg slowly started to swing rhythmically like a metronome as she became more comfortable talking with the women.

The twins would have normally exchanged glances upon discovering that it may be that Ruby was found at her and Levi's secret spot, but they both noticed that Grace was feeling more relaxed and wanted her to continue.

Grace continued, "I'm surprised Levi told you about their secret. I'm not even sure that he knows that Ruby told me about it. I was thinking that his conscience feels pretty heavy about that now that she is gone. I mean, Bishop Packer and Mr. Mast would be furious, even now, if they found out."

Before the twins could have explained that it wasn't Levi that told them about the secret meetings, Grace continued, "But what I wanted to tell you - and the thing I don't know who to tell - is that Ruby was scared. The week before she died - or maybe it was two weeks, I'm not sure - Ruby kept feeling like someone was following her, or watching her. She couldn't pin it, but she was sure it was happening. One time, when she was walking from her father's barn to her house, she heard a sound - I think she said it sounded like a twig broke or something. She stopped and turned around, but it was almost dark so she couldn't see really well. She felt like someone was there. And really close. She said she ran to the door, but once she got there, she thought she heard the motor of a car close by. She told her *maem*, but her *maem* didn't believe her."

"Then another time, she was laying in bed about to drift off to sleep when she saw a small round light reflection shining on the wall next to the bed. She was facing the wall and she said that the light was on her bed and then moved to the wall, and she thought it was coming from her window. She turned around to see if someone was shining a light in her window and the light went away, like it was just turned off. She ran to her *maem* and *dat*'s room, but again, her *maem* said she was imagining things."

Grace stopped and said, "I don't mean to say anything disrespectful for Mrs. Packer. I told Ruby that she was a good *maem*, and to be honest, Ruby did have a good imagination."

The twins nodded, and Anna said, "*Ja*, Mrs. Packer loved Ruby very much. Did Ruby ever see anything more than that, Grace?"

"I'm not sure. I feel like she said that it happened more than that, but I can't remember exactly now. But, she was frightened, and now I'm frightened that she may have been right.. and if I don't tell this secret to someone, this person might hurt someone else," Grace's nerves and fear were starting to build inside her again. She fidgeted, struggling to sit still on the bench, and begged, "What should I do? Should I tell Mrs. Packer? Can you please help me tell her? I don't want to say the wrong thing, and I'm so nervous about that. And I'm scared." She covered her face with her hands as her tears returned.

Beth moved over to sit next to her and draped her arm around her shoulders. "Everything will be okay, Grace. I promise. We will talk to Mrs. Packer. Please don't worry. You did the right thing. *Denki* for telling us. We will need to tell the sheriff this information, though, so that he can do a thorough investigation. He might want to ask you some questions about it, but he is a very kind man and you can trust him."

Anna chimed in, "*Ja*, and we can be there to help support you, too, if you'd like."

Grace uncovered her face and leaned into Beth's embrace. "I would like that very much," she said, speaking barely above a whisper.

"Ok, then," said Beth, her voice at a higher pitch. "Let's go back in before everyone starts to wonder where we've gone," Beth chuckled and gave Grace one last squeeze.

Anna reached over and wiped Grace's face with her linen handkerchief and squeezed her hand. "Everything is going to be okay, Grace. It is *Gotte's* will."

Grace nodded. She felt such a sense of relief after speaking with the women. The women rose to go in, Anna leaning on her cane. Grace straightened her *kapp* and rubbed her palms down the sides of her dress. Entering the Packer's house through the side door, no one seemed to notice they were gone. Grace thanked Anna and Beth one more time and headed off to find her friends. Beth pulled Anna aside and whispered, "I wonder if we should have asked Grace about the deputy."

"I didn't have the heart to put her through anymore storytelling or questions. We can leave that up to the sheriff,"

Anna said firmly, looking at Beth with a stern look in her eye. She knew Beth wanted to solve the case without the sheriff, but Anna wasn't sure that was going to be smart, or even necessary.

Beth registered the look and knew exactly what Anna meant. She decided not to challenge it. This wasn't the time or place to discuss the details of how Ruby was killed. She was willing to put a pin in it. For now. But this conversation wasn't over.

Chapter Sixteen

"Yes, ma'am. Okay. No, I am listening, and I will follow up on it. Thank you for calling." Mark Streen replaced the old phone earpiece back into its cradle and sat back in his chair, a heavy sigh escaped his lips.

Deputy Chase Brown set his cellphone down on his desk in front of him and looked over at the sheriff. "Everything ok?" he asked.

"Yeah, it's fine. That was Shirley Hatfield. She and her husband own the flower shop in town. She said she overheard the drifter talking to himself outside her shop this morning saying that he killed Ruby Packer in the woods.

I'll tell ya, everyone thinks they are a detective in this town. Everyone has a theory. But, you said that you saw that guy the night Ruby went missing - and you can't have a better alibi than the deputy himself. Plus, where would he even hide her? He simply couldn't mastermind something like that." Sheriff Streen ran his hands through his hair. The lack of sleep showed on his face.

Chase nodded. "Yeah, I'm with you. There's no way that guy killed Ruby. He was probably just muttering something to himself. Everyone is on edge, so the florist's wife must've just heard what she wanted to hear. We don't have any real leads, though. We have to be missing something. I think we might need to come to terms with it being some random murder by someone passing through town."

Mark looked over at Chase and shook his head. "I don't think so. Something in my gut tells me it's someone here in town. The autopsy report showed bruises around her ankle as if she was bound in some way - but not with rope. Maybe it was metal and she was chained to something somewhere, but she didn't look like she had spent any time in a dungeon or anything like that. She didn't have any drugs in her system. She died of an epileptic seizure. No signs of trauma. Nothing under her fingernails. The body left us no clues to go on except for that mark and bruise on her ankle. I'm stumped."

"We're missing something," said Chase.

"Yes, definitely. We can tell that she was well-cared for in custody. Whoever took her must have cared deeply for her, maybe even treasured her. I think I'm going to go visit Hank Davis today. There's something about that guy that I can't quite put my finger on. He seems to have some weird fascination with the Amish community, so I don't think it would hurt to check his alibi. Do you mind holding down the fort until I get back? I don't want to miss an important phone call with a lead." The sheriff stood and stretched his back, arms reaching toward the ceiling.

"Yep. I can do that. Let me know if you end up needing backup once you get to Davis' place. He definitely seems like trouble." Chase wished he could ride along with the sheriff. He wasn't optimistic that any new leads would be coming into the office, but he was still too green on the job to challenge anything his boss asked him to do.

The sheriff had one arm in his coat when he heard the sound of a horse's hooves on the pavement out in front of his office. Glancing out the window, he saw the twins securing their horse and buggy to the post. They were up the porch steps and through the door in a flash.

"Sheriff, I'm glad you're here. We have something to show you," the twins spoke. Their identical faces showed that they were there on business. Each grabbed a visitor chair from in front of the window and pulled them close to the sheriff's desk. Beth nodded to the deputy, acknowledging his presence, but neither of the sisters had come to speak to him. It was the sheriff they wanted to speak with and share what they had just learned.

"Hello, Mrs. Troyer and Mrs. Miller. How are you?" Sheriff Streen had removed his arm from his coat and sat back down, pencil in hand, hovering over a blank yellow pad of paper. He had hoped that what the sisters were bringing him today was better than anything else he had been hearing.

"If you don't mind, Sheriff, we're just going to get right to it and tell you why we're here," Anna said, the words rushing out of her mouth. "We visited Margaret Packer yesterday, and she gave us Ruby's diary."

Beth pulled the diary out of her quilted handbag. It was a small notebook, plain on the outside. She held it in her hands gingerly.

Anna continued, excited to share their findings and their suspicion, "Ruby was being followed. Her best friend, Grace Schwartz, confirmed that Ruby had been uneasy, feeling as if someone was watching her the last few days of her life. Ruby and Levi Mast had been meeting secretly in the woods, and we think whoever was following her, knew this and grabbed her while she was there." Anna took a deep breath.

"Levi was meeting her secretly in the woods? What do you mean by that?" Sheriff Streen asked, slightly raising an eyebrow. His hand was still on the writing pad.

Beth interjected, "Levi and Ruby were having a secret love affair, we found out. Grace confirmed it. They were meeting out in the woods near a stream and a field of wildflowers. It was very innocent, but it had to be in secret because Ruby was not given permission by her parents to date just yet."

"That's beside the point, though, Sheriff," Anna interrupted sternly. "The point is that Ruby was being followed. By a stranger. Her secret meetings with Levi just opened up the opportunity for the stranger to take her." Anna looked over at Beth and exchanged worried looks. This conversation was not going as planned and was taking a turn in the wrong direction. The Mast family was a respectable family in the community and they knew Levi to be a happy, kind young man. They didn't for one second think he had anything to do with Ruby's demise.

The sheriff reached out for the diary. "May I see the diary, please, ma'am?" he asked politely. Beth handed the notebook to him hesitantly. The room fell silent as he reviewed a few pages, starting at the back of the book with the more recent entries. "What else do you know about this innocent love affair? What exactly did Grace say about Ruby and Levi's relationship? Did anyone else know about their secret meetings?"

What have we done? thought Anna. Her mind was racing. Her instincts were telling her that Levi was not Ruby's killer, yet she may have just presented all the evidence needed to make him suspect number one in the eyes of the law. Until just now, she hadn't made the connection that Levi had never told anyone since Ruby's disappearance about their affair; that he had found Ruby's dead body in their secret meeting place; and then there were the comments made by Grace and by Ruby herself in her own diary that Levi was more invested in their relationship than Ruby was. *Ach du lieva*, Anna thought, she needed to fix this.

As if again reading her sister's thoughts, Beth responded to the sheriff's questions and said, "We only know what we've told you and what's in the diary, Sheriff. We believe the killer was watching Ruby and followed her out to the woods and grabbed her when Levi wasn't there." And then, as if she had almost forgotten, she said quickly, "And we also spoke with Jessica McLean. She owns the diner in town, and she said that..." Beth stopped and looked over at Chase.

Chase met her eyes with a blank expression and said, "Please do go on, Mrs. Troyer. What did Jessica say?"

Beth felt the hair raise on her arms. She immediately looked back at the sheriff and grabbed Anna's hand. Was the deputy mocking her? Challenging her to tell the sheriff about how he had been rejected by Ruby? She wondered if Sheriff Streen even knew that story. She continued as if the deputy weren't in the room, and said, "Ms. McLean said that Samuel Graber and Hank Davis have been telling a few people that it's the community's fault that you shut down the games in his establishment. And they have threatened us with revenge."

The sheriff sighed and responded with a kind voice, "I'm so sorry to hear that, Mrs. Troyer and Mrs. Miller. I will definitely talk to both of them and ask them what they know about Ruby's disappearance. If they are behind this at all, I will get to the bottom of it." He paused for a moment and set the pen down on the pad carefully, next to the closed notebook. "Unfortunately, I am also going to have to talk to Levi again, as well." Seeing the look on the women's faces, he continued, "Please don't worry. I realize that Levi is young and I will be sure to include his parents and speak with respect when I am asking him about the affair. I can only assume that his own parents do not know about this either. And you may be right, Levi may have nothing to do with Ruby's death, but right now, he is the only suspect that we have considering the evidence."

"Oh, please, Sheriff, we are positive it wasn't Levi. He is a boy with morals, a hard worker, and he has such promise. Something like this could ruin his future and his family's reputation in the community if it were to get out. Please. If you are going to approach him, please do so discreetly. For the sake of his family." Anna paused and then looked over in the deputy's direction. She thought she caught a glimpse of a smirk on Chase's face that disappeared just before anyone else could see it. Meeting and holding her gaze with the deputy confidently, she spoke, "I'm afraid we may be uncovering a few more secrets in Little Valley before this is all said and done."

The sheriff was focused on his notepad, adding details to remember to ask Levi about. His left hand held the diary propped open on his desk to the last written page. He mumbled, "Oh, I think you may be right, ma'am. I think you may be right."

Chapter Seventeen

After seeing the sisters to their buggy and thanking them for coming in, Sheriff Mark Streen returned to the office to gather his things.

Deputy Chase was holding Ruby's diary, thumbing through the pages. He wasn't looking for clues. He was looking for any mention of his own encounters with the girl. So far, he had found nothing. He hadn't told anyone about his fascination with her, but he was more overcome with a sense of grave disappointment. He just knew there had to be a diary entry about the day the two of them met and how Ruby was smitten at first sight.

"Well, I don't mean to interrupt you," the sheriff said teasingly, "but I'm gonna head out to go talk to Levi. I'll talk to him and his dad on their farm this time and try to keep things low key like I promised Mrs. Miller and Mrs. Troyer."

Chase looked up. "I don't know why you don't just bring him on in. My bet is on that horse, for sure. Young or not, he's the one with the motive and the means."

"Yeah, but I'm not sure he is the mastermind we're looking for either. His youth is a problem. It brings up the same question - where would he have kept her? I'm hoping to get some answers, and I'm not ruling him out, but it just doesn't feel right either." Sheriff Streen set his cowboy hat on his head and before he left, he joked, "Don't get so caught up in that girl's diary that you don't hear the phone ring."

Chase chuckled and responded, "Yeah, good luck with the boy. Ask the right questions and the truth will probably come pouring out of that kid. You'll probably have the case closed by sundown."

The sheriff walked down the steps and sat in his patrol car. He took a deep breath as he started the ignition. *Surely, this boy couldn't have killed that poor girl,* he thought. One thing is for sure: he didn't want to believe it.

The five mile drive to the Mast's family farm felt like one of the longest drives of his life. His mind was running at top speed as he was remembering Ruby's notes in her diary about how Levi's feelings were stronger than hers. Besides the fact that they were meeting secretly, and that he had ironically found her body in their favorite meeting spot, it was that one sentence that he couldn't let go.

The sheriff pulled up to the Mast home. The large home was painted a light blue with gray shutters. The house was an Americana style with an open covered porch that wrapped around all sides. A lazy orange tabby cat was taking a nap on one of the cushioned seats on the porch in a ray of sunshine. A brown hound dog sporting a grayed snout raised his head from his lounging position just a few feet away from the porch. He let out a muffled bark that was more like a grumble as the sheriff's boots touched the driveway. The sheriff approached the front door and the excited barks of a smaller dog could be heard from inside, either warning the family or welcoming the guest - the sheriff couldn't quite tell. Either way, the barks were followed by the sight of Mrs. Mast standing in the doorway, holding the door open.

"Well, hello, Sheriff Streen. What brings you out this way?" She asked with a warm smile. Her voice hid any concern she was feeling, but her deep brown eyes couldn't help but tell the truth.

The sheriff remained at the bottom of the porch steps, removed his hat, and replied, "Hi, Mrs. Mast. My apologies for the unannounced visit, but I was wondering if Levi and Mr. Mast were around?"

"They should be in the barn, or just out behind it, Sheriff. There's lots of work preparing for the winter right now, so they've kept busy. You can go on back there, if you'd like. Can I bring you some iced tea or anything while you're here?" She asked, fighting to keep her voice from shaking. Levi had just started to eat again after a couple of days, and she noticed that he seemed a little more rested this morning. She was so worried that he wasn't yet ready to talk about what he saw on the day he found Ruby - and that it might send him a few steps back in his recovery.

"No thank you, ma'am. I won't be here long. Just checking in on things." Sheriff Streen had hoped the words would put her mind at ease. He felt compassion for her, knowing how emotionally distraught Levi was the last time he had seen him. He knew it must be hard for a parent to see their child suffer.

Becca nodded and watched as the sheriff made his way down the stone path toward the barn behind the house. She closed the door and returned to the kitchen. She said a prayer for *Gotte's* protection over Levi before she continued to peel potatoes.

The sheriff entered the barn. Both sliding doors at the front and at the back of the barn were pushed open creating a sort of corridor through the horse stables. The sheriff called out, "Nathan?" When no one answered right away, he continued through the barn and called out, "Levi? It's Sheriff Streen."

Nathan Mast poked his head out into the back opening and said, "Sheriff Streen. Hi, there. We're just back here. Come on back."

The sheriff exited the back door of the barn to find Levi and his father hard at work. They were both wearing rubber boots up to their knees and were elbows deep washing out the troughs used to store their animals' feed. Two pitchforks and three shovels of varying heights leaned against the back barn wall, sparkling clean. The ground was wet so the sheriff was careful where he stood. He reached out to shake hands with Nathan first, then Levi.

"Hi, fellas," said Sheriff Streen. "You two look like you've been working hard. Can you take a break for a few minutes to chat? I've got a few things I want to share with you." Streen tried as hard as he could to make the conversation sound lighthearted. He didn't want to go into this with a closed mind or come across intimidating in any way.

Levi looked at his dad with a worried look. His stomach turned and he grumbled something that the sheriff couldn't quite make out. Nathan gave Levi a cross look, as if it were a warning, then turned to the sheriff with a half smile. "Sure thing, Sheriff. Wanna just take a seat in the sun on those hay bales?" He gestured to a collection of four single bales that sat next to a tall pile stacked neatly.

"Perfect," said the sheriff, making his way over to the closest one and taking a seat. The father and son followed right behind him and sat across from him, next to each other.

"Levi, how are you feeling? The last time I saw you, well, you weren't feeling so good. I'm sorry about that whole thing. I was hoping that taking you down to the office might make you feel safe - but I don't think it had that impact on you at all." The sheriff noticed how Levi's shoulders were starting to relax and lower down below his ears a bit, so he had hoped he was building trust.

"Honestly, the reason I'm here is to find out more about Ruby. You see, the investigation into her death is still going strong and I'm asking everyone I can to share anything they know to see if I can get a clue. As a matter of fact, after this, I'm headed to the Schwartz home to talk to Grace since she was Ruby's best friend and all." The sheriff noticed Levi's shoulders get tight again. He began to fidget, moving around as if he couldn't sit still. The sheriff figured Levi knew that Grace knew about the secret meetings, and Levi's reaction confirmed that suspicion.

Nathan noticed the change in his son's demeanor, too. He reached out and put a hand on his shoulder, "Son, let's just tell the sheriff the good things you remember about Ruby. That's what he wants to hear. Tell the sheriff about your friendship and the things you two liked to talk about. What kind of things were her favorite things?"

"That's right, Levi. I have all I need to know about the day you found her. I'm just looking to get to know Ruby better, and I know the two of you were friends." The sheriff nodded and smiled a warm smile at the boy.

The expression on Levi's face was one of distress. He burst into tears and roughly wiped them away with the backs of his hands. "*Dat*, I have to tell you something," Levi said, sobbing. He pushed his dad's hand away and stood on his feet. "Ruby was more than a friend," he shouted. "She was going to be my wife! We loved each other. We were secretly meeting in the woods so we could spend time together. We were hiding everything because she wasn't supposed to be seein' anyone yet. The bishop was very strict about that. But we loved each other!" Levi cried as he uttered each word. The sheriff could see spit spray into the air from his lips as he spoke.

Levi continued, his hands down by his sides. He stomped his foot like a toddler and cried, "And now we can't ever be together! She's gone forever! My heart is broken and I couldn't tell anyone! I'll never love anyone more than I loved her!" He threw himself down onto the bale of hay as if it were a mattress, his face resting on his bent arm, his body heaving from the sobs.

Nathan sat there in complete shock, unable to speak for a moment. He looked at the sheriff, his eyes begging for answers, but the sheriff waited to respond or say anything.

"Son," Nathan said. Levi continued to sob, face down in the hay. Nathan reached out and touched his back. "Son, I'm sorry. I had no idea. Please, son, sit up. There is a lot more to talk about here." His voice was weak and trembling. He was putting the pieces together in his head slowly. This is why the sheriff is visiting again. Levi found Ruby's body in the woods - and that's where they had been meeting, secretly, behind everyone's back.

Nathan looked at the sheriff as Levi continued to weep. He had put the puzzle together. His boy was in trouble.

Chapter Eighteen

"Thank you for meeting with me today," Matthew Beiler said, his brow furrowed and his chin lifted. Matthew stood with Hank Davis in the front parlor of the farmhouse style bed-and-breakfast, finally face to face with the owner.

A quilt made with shades of red, white and purple hung on the wall next to the door leading to the dining area. There was a simple brick fireplace on one wall, a basket filled with cut pieces of wood was set on the hearth. A simple evergreen wreath hung on the bricks above the fireplace. There was a sofa with wood trim that bordered a woven fabric of neutral colors. A colorful braided rug lay on the hardwood floor floating in front of the sofa. A pair of beautifully crafted rocking chairs sat together in front of the picture window that ran from ceiling to floor.

Hank had postponed this meeting as long as he could - but now, he was ready to have the meeting and move on. He wasn't fond of the Amish and he was especially confused about what he knew about this guy, Matthew Beiler. Matthew dressed like them, but he didn't have a beard. Hank couldn't understand why anyone would want to come back to that lifestyle after living like normal people for a few years, and then on the flip side of that, he questioned why the community even allowed him to come back after that long. Regardless, he was annoyed that those people had sent Matthew as their spokesperson. He was no idiot - he knew it was because Matthew had experience outside of the community. He was far from impressed though. No one was even really sure what Matthew had done for a living before he returned.

One thing Hank knew for sure was that ever since he had decided to open a bed-and-breakfast in Little Valley, the Amish people had been up in arms about it. They were trying to stop him from making money off the tourism boom that the town had seen, and they were just plain ig-norant to think that they could keep all the benefits of that to themselves. He had watched those people try to take down his friend's bar. Samuel Graber had to remove the gaming in his bar, and it didn't take a genius to see who was behind that. Hank would not let them impede his business growth, though. He had already started fighting back. He was pretty sure that was why this joke of a man stood in front of him now. *Game on*, he thought to himself. He stiffened his posture, his arms crossed in front of his chest.

"Nice place you have here," Matthew said, interrupting Hank's thoughts.

"Yeah?" Hank asked, raising an eyebrow. "What is the purpose of your visit today, Mr. Beiler? I don't have time to pretend like we're friends."

Matthew hesitated to answer but maintained eye contact. His tongue ran along the inside bottom of his lip and he drew in a breath. "Why can't we be friends, Mr. Davis?" Matthew asked but his eyes were not friendly.

Hank scoffed. "I tried to give y'all a chance to share in the big profits that this place is going to make, but y'all didn't want nothing to do with it. Maybe you should go back to your little Amish town and get caught up on the actual facts of why we're not gonna be friends, *Mr. Beiler*," Hank responded angrily, moving his neck and head back and forth as he emphasized Matthew's name.

Matthew refused to be provoked. "Well, then, there must be some kind of misunderstanding. One proverb we live by says *'Our duty is not to see through one another, but to see one another through.'* We don't want to share in your profits, but we do wish you well."

Hank put his hand under his chin, overacting as if he were deep in thought. "Hmmm... then I wonder why we're meeting." He crossed his arms again, and feeling annoyed, he said, "Please enlighten me. Why exactly are you wasting my time right now? And you can cut out the riddles."

Remaining calm, Matthew responded, "I want to bury the hatchet. Make amends. Start fresh." He reached out his hand for a handshake and said, "What d'ya say? Can we start over?"

Hank didn't shake his hand. "I'll tell you what, you go back home and tell your people that if they want to be friends," Hank lifted his hands and moved the first two fingers on each hand to imply that he was putting quotations around the word 'friends,' "then, they can agree to sell me their goods at cost so I can resale them in my storefront when I open. Ya know, we can consider it a friend discount." He winked at Matthew.

"I see," Matthew said, lowering his outstretched hand. "Well, the thing is that we're not really in the wholesale business, and to be honest, your customers would be our customers at the market. We provide for our families with the income we make on our goods and selling at your proposed friend discount takes away from that and in some cases might cost us in the end. It's just not good business, you understand."

Hank shrugged. He couldn't care less what worked for them. He doubted they knew much about business anyway. The Amish lifestyle fascinated the tourists, and his plan was to replicate that for his guests the best way he could to draw more visitors. "Well, I guess I could buy at a price just above cost. Still at a discount, though. But then, y'all are gonna have to raise your prices at the market so I still have the best price here in my storefront. I would sign that contract."

"Why would we do that, Mr. Davis? Again, that makes little sense for us. We would be happy to sell you items in bulk, at bulk pricing, and then you can price them however you like. But we will remain in control of our retail pricing." Matthew's patience was clearly waning.

"I'll think about it," Hank said as he reached out and slapped Matthew's arm, "and y'all should think about it, too. Y'all aren't used to competition out here in Little Valley, but it's here now - and this is only the beginning." Hank spoke with condescension, "Sometimes in business, we have to do things we don't want to do, just to stay alive. It can get pretty ruthless, I'll tell ya. There can be some hard lessons to learn, but maybe you've got a few more proverbs to help y'all through it."

"Okay, you think about it then," Matthew responded, ignoring Hank's attempt to ruffle his feathers. "I'm sure I'll be seeing you around town." He tipped his hat and headed toward the door.

"Yep. I'm sure we'll see each other again," Hank replied, following him. "I'll be opening the doors here in just a few weeks, so y'all still have a little bit of time to think about it. Maybe I'll come see you next time."

Matthew stopped a few steps outside the door, his foot on the edge of the welcome mat. He turned around and said, "Please do come visit sometime. I'd be happy to show you around." But the look on his face didn't convey the same message.

Just as Matthew untied his horse and mounted his buggy, the sheriff's vehicle arrived and parked in the small lot next to the bed-and-breakfast. Sheriff Streen parked in the parking space next to the one that had a sign with the image of a horse and buggy with the words, 'Amish Buggy Parking Only. Violators will have to walk.' Hank wondered if the sheriff thought it was funny. Since he had stuck that signpost in the ground, he had never seen anyone park there.

The sheriff tipped his hat to Matthew as he approached the porch, and Matthew returned the greeting before heading down the street.

"Howdy, Sheriff," Hank said. "What brings you here today? Running a permit check?"

"Why? You got gaming tables set up inside or something?" The sheriff responded, letting Hank know he caught that innuendo.

Hank gestured for the sheriff to enter the front door, leading to the parlor. "Wanna have a seat, Sheriff?" He asked, secretly hoping the answer was no.

"Actually, I wouldn't mind a tour of the place, Hank. I haven't seen the inside of your operation just yet," the sheriff said, removing his cowboy hat.

"Ah, well, you might just have to wait for the rest of the public. The rooms aren't all ready yet. I'll let you know, though. Heck, I'll even give ya a sneak peek a day or two before opening day, if you'd like." Hank paused briefly before continuing, "Is that why you stopped by? To see the unfinished rooms?"

"Well, I also just wanted to check in on you, Hank. See how things are going. I've been hearing a few rumors that you've been pretty unhappy with some of the recent happenings in Little Valley, and I thought maybe I could help you work that out." The sheriff looked Hank dead in the eye.

Although Hank didn't care for Sheriff Mark Streen, the last thing he wanted was trouble from the law. "I don't know anything about these rumors you're referring to, Sheriff. I've been pretty focused on getting my place restored and ready to open. I haven't been paying much attention to anything else that is happening around Little Valley, to be honest."

The sheriff nodded and asked casually, "Where are you living at, Hank, when you're not working?"

"I live here. I have a suite in the back of the house. Why?" Hank was starting to feel uneasy.

"Oh, I'm just curious. Maybe you could show me that room?" Hank felt the sheriff's eyes drilling through his own.

"Well, you're gonna have to have a better reason than curiosity to see my room, Sheriff. I mean, I'm curious how your car drives, but I'm not asking to take it on a test drive, am I? What's the meaning of this? Get to the point." Hank was ready for this conversation to end, but he had a feeling Sheriff Streen was just getting started.

"I got nothing to hide, Hank. It would be a strange request, but I would be happy to let you take my cruiser on a test drive if you asked nicely." The sheriff chuckled.

Hank straightened up and stepped closer to the sheriff, his shoulders back and his chest puffed. "I have no interest in driving your car, Sheriff. Get to the point and ask me what you came here to ask."

Without hesitation, the Sheriff said, "I'm sure you've heard about the Amish girl who was found dead in the woods across town. I was just wondering where you were last Sunday night, a week ago, Hank?"

Hank felt a knot forming in his stomach, but he fought for his face not to show it. "I'm pretty sure I was at Samuel Graber's bar until closing, and then I came home. Here. I came here and went right to sleep. Early the next morning, I met with some contractors to get started working on the landscaping out back. I would be more than happy to get you their contact info, if you need it."

The two men stood less than a foot apart, staring at each other for what felt to Hank like an eternity. Finally, the sheriff spoke, "Sure, I'll take their info and I'll just double check that timing with Samuel, as well. I intended to stop by and say hello to our friend anyway."

Hank reached into his back pocket and scrolled through his phone until he found the landscaping company's information. Sheriff Streen jotted the information down in a small notebook he kept in his front pocket. Hank saw that his hand was shaking slightly, and he hoped the sheriff didn't notice that, too. Hank closed his phone and said, "And say hello to *our friend*, Samuel, for me, will ya? I haven't seen him in a few days."

"Yep," said the sheriff, as he placed his cowboy hat back on his head. "Alright then, since I have to wait for the grand tour, I guess I'll just let myself out. Nice talking with you." The sheriff turned around, his hand on the inside of the door and said, "Oh, and before I forget. I'll need you to stay in town until I can confirm your story. And some advice: If you want to fit in here, maybe show some more respect to those who were here long before you moved in. You'll catch more flies with honey than with vinegar, you know."

Hank nodded. "Have a good day now, Sheriff." Hank muttered sarcastically. He shut the heavy front door and exhaled. *Last thing I want to do is fit in with those freaks*, he thought. He wiped the beads of sweat that rested on the back of his neck. He hated that he let the sheriff get under his skin like that.

Hank walked to the kitchen and pulled the refrigerator door open. He grabbed a cold beer and popped it open using the built-in bottle cap opener fastened to the side of the refrigerator-freezer unit. He took a big gulp and then headed back into the parlor to relax, locking the basement door as he passed it.

Chapter Nineteen

―――――◆○◆―――――

"Should we go see Moses after we drop off the cinnamon rolls to Mr. Hatfield?" Anna asked Beth. Beth was holding the reins in her hands, her eyes forward on the road in front of them.

"*Ja*, that sounds good to me. I haven't seen his shop in a long time. After that, I need to pick up a few things at the grocery, if we have time." Beth said. Beth couldn't stop thinking about Ruby and her disappearance. The sisters had not heard any news about an arrest yet, and Anna made Beth promise that for just one day, she would take a break and not speak of it. The sisters had questioned everyone that they could - except for Samuel and Hank Davis, but their husbands had pulled the plug on that, saying the two men were too dangerous. The sheriff had assured them he would follow up with them. Anna said it was time to let him and the deputy take the lead now.

Beth also wondered about Levi and his family. She had been saying extra prayers for them ever since the sisters brought the diary to the sheriff. The sheriff said he was going to go meet with Levi and Nathan Mast that day, but they had yet to hear anything at all about the conversation. She hoped Levi was absolved from suspicion and that the sheriff had moved on to the next person on the list of suspects.

Beth pulled up to the tie in front of Moses' hardware shop and secured the horse there. She preferred to park there since he was family and the parking spot gave a little bit more grace to those like herself who weren't that skilled at parking. Anna handed the box of cinnamon rolls to Beth to hold while she carefully stepped out of the buggy. She reached back in to grab her cane.

"You'll be done with that cane in no time, *Schwester*," said Beth.

"*Ja*, I have my doctor's appointment next week, and I've been putting more and more weight on my leg without any pain. The cane is starting to feel like it's just in the way now." Anna said. They chuckled together.

"It's going to take more than that to hold my sister down, I'll tell you what," said Beth, smiling.

"Well, let's hope there aren't any more accidents worse than that in my future," said Anna, winking at Beth.

The two headed into the flower shop. They wanted to give Mr. Hatfield a box of cinnamon rolls to thank him for the beautiful flower arrangement he brought over on the day of Moses' celebration.

The women stopped to admire the displays of beautiful tulips, tiger lilies and roses just inside the door of the shop. They hadn't been in the shop more than a minute when they heard raised voices coming from the back office. Beth grabbed Anna's arm just as Anna opened her mouth to announce their presence and raised her finger to her lips.

"They're gonna find out, Henry, and I will not go to jail because of your stupid decisions," the female voice could be heard across the shop.

Beth and Anna looked at each other, wide-eyed and frozen. They knew they shouldn't be eavesdropping. Anna felt a pit in her stomach.

"Shirley, they're not going to find out. There is no way they'll even suspect us, and besides, we'll be gone in just a few days and I've arranged for all traces to be erased. It's not like we haven't done this before." It was Mr. Hatfield's voice. The sisters recognized the voice instantly.

Beth gasped and Anna clasped a hand over her sister's mouth.

"That's the problem, Henry. I'm getting too old to keep running away because of your mistakes. I really liked it in Decatur, and I was starting to like Little Valley, too. Don't do me any more favors. How about you stop bringing me presents that I didn't ask for? It wasn't even my birthday and what a ridiculous connection that her name was the same as my birthstone." Her tone was demeaning and cruel.

The sisters couldn't believe what they were hearing. Could they be talking about Ruby? Did Mr. Hatfield take Ruby, and why would he do that?

The sound of packing tape stretching and then being cut drifted out of the office. Beth thought it was the perfect time for the twins to escape without being noticed, but the sound of footsteps approaching soon followed.

Anna opened and re-shut the door hard. "Hello? Mr. Hatfield?" She called out, sounding cheery. Beth instantly knew to play along.

Mr. Hatfield entered the front of the shop just seconds later, his face flushed and his hair disheveled. A look of surprise crossed his face. He smiled at the women and greeted them with a tone louder than normal, "Hello, Mrs. Miller and Mrs. Troyer."

Anna continued to act as if the twins had just arrived and noticed nothing unusual. "Hi, there! Beth and I came by to drop off some of our famous butterscotch cinnamon rolls to show our appreciation for the lovely flower arrangement you brought by the house for Moses' celebration. That was so kind, and we really do appreciate it. The cinnamon rolls are from our whole family, including Moses and Sarah."

Mr. Hatfield composed himself and said, "Ah, yes, that's very nice. You didn't have to do that, but my wife loves sweets, so I am sure she will enjoy these." He took the box into his hands and set it on the counter. "Is there anything else I can do for you today?"

"No, thank you, Mr. Hatfield. We'll let you get back to business. We just wanted to stop by for a minute." Anna responded, calm as a cucumber.

Beth interjected, "Yes, we have to pick up a few things at the grocery while we're out. Please do tell Mrs. Hatfield that we said hello." There was no sound at all coming from the back office. Either Mrs. Hatfield was hiding in silence or she had slipped out a back door.

"Absolutely, I will tell her you stopped by. Have a good day and thank you again!" Mr. Hatfield smiled.

The twins turned to leave, waving goodbye and complimenting the flowers on the way out the door. As soon as the door shut behind them, the sisters hugged each other, shaken from what they had just witnessed.

Anna exclaimed in a loud whisper, "Dear *Gotte*, this can't be true!"

Beth nodded and squeezed Anna's hands, "I think we just got the clue we've been looking for, *Schwester*. But let's slow down. Are we sure we heard what we think we heard?" It was all so shocking. They knew that Mr. Hatfield was peculiar, but what if they misunderstood the conversation? Accusing someone of kidnapping and murder was not to be taken lightly. "Should we go to the library and see if we can find out anything before we tell the sheriff?"

Moses spotted the sisters on the sidewalk in front of his shop and came outside to greet them. "Well, *hallo, Maem* and Aunt Beth! *Wie discht?*" As soon as his feet hit the threshold of his store, he felt like he might be interrupting a heavy conversation. "Everything ok?" Moses asked. As he got closer he noticed the women looked as if they had just seen a ghost.

"*Ja*, Moses, we're fine," said Anna, looking back at Hatfield's flower shop. Turning back to Beth, she lowered her voice again and said, "I don't want to waste any time. We don't know if they know we heard them or not. They could be getting ready to leave town right now." She turned to her son-in-law, "Moses, can you drive me to the sheriff's office? It's an emergency." Without waiting for an answer, she said, "*Schwester*, you go ahead to the library in your buggy and then meet us at the sheriff's office. Please hurry."

Beth nodded and moved quickly. As she was climbing into her buggy, Anna took Moses's arm and led him into his shop. Moses was confused, but sensed the urgency, and he trusted his mother-in-law and aunt completely. Moses moved quickly to close his shop as Anna stood at the front door, wringing her hands and waiting.

Beth arrived at the town's small library within just a few minutes. She parked the buggy and tied the horse to the post out front, and bounded up the stairs to the front door of the library. She almost ran into Mr. Wilson who was leaving the library, keys in hand.

"Oh my goodness," said Mr. Wilson as he saw Beth. She was certainly on a mission. "I was just closing up," he said as Beth rushed past him and headed toward the back of the library.

"I'll just be a minute," Beth yelled out as she headed toward the microfiche readers.

Mr. Wilson was a kind man, about the same age as Beth and Anna. He had opened the town's library with the inheritance left to him by his family. He loved books - the way they smelled, the way they felt, the way they lined up on the shelves. He was an avid reader himself, and he enjoyed recommending books to anyone interested. Since his wife had passed a few years ago, he took comfort in his little library more so than ever before. He had a small farm of his own and he would share the extra fresh eggs and vegetables with folk who would come in to borrow a book.

Over the years of growing up in the same town, the sisters considered Greg Wilson and his late wife friends. Despite a crush Mr. Wilson had on Anna years before, he always struggled to tell the two sisters apart. When he would run into them, he would try to guess, but more often than not, he would guess wrong. So, he wondered which sister had just passed him in such a rush just now. It was uncommon to see one sister without the other, and he followed her to see if he could help find anything.

Walking up to Beth, he said, "Is that you, Anna? Or Beth? You know, I'm never sure."

Beth was distracted, but she answered, "It's Beth. Ok, this is going to sound strange, but I'm looking for newspaper articles, or anything you can find, about the disappearance and even murder of young children in Decatur happening about a year ago. It has to be an unsolved crime."

Greg took over Beth's spot at the reader, adjusted his glasses and began scrolling through pages of newspapers while Beth looked over his shoulder. They were traveling back much further than a year ago at this point and Beth was just about to give up when Greg stopped at an article with a photo of a man and woman with a young girl. The girl looked to be about twelve years old. She had beautiful features with long blonde hair, but she wasn't smiling.

"Wait. Is that Mr. and Mrs. Hatfield?" Greg asked, shocked. Beth nodded. She was speechless, busy reading the article. The headline read, 'Young girl disappears into thin air. Parents offer a reward.' The date on the article went back almost ten years.

Greg jumped up. "Let me grab it off the printer," he said, rushing to the front desk. Beth followed right behind him. He handed her the printed article and wished her luck. He had quickly packed up a few fresh eggs in a soft cloth bag while the page was printing. Once she had what she needed, Beth thanked him for his help and headed out the door. She needed to meet Anna and Moses at the sheriff's office as soon as possible. Greg waved goodbye to Beth, calling out, "Please be safe, Beth!"

About fifteen minutes later, Beth pulled up at the sheriff's office and hurried inside. Beth and Moses were sitting in the chairs in front of Sheriff Streen's desk. Both the sheriff and Deputy Chase were on the phone - Sheriff Streen was using the landline and Deputy Brown was talking on his cellphone.

"Yes. Hatfield. Do you have any record of a couple living there named Shirley and Henry Hatfield?" Beth could hear a bit of excitement in the young deputy's voice.

And from the sheriff, Beth heard, "I'm looking for any female young teen murders in the area."

Beth squatted down between Moses and Anna's chairs and held out the printed article for them to see. The paper was slightly crumpled as Beth had shoved it into her handbag during the rush to get to the sheriff's office. Moses jumped up and offered Beth his seat.

"*Denki*, Moses," Beth said as she turned the chair to directly face Anna. Moses moved to hover between the two of them and Beth said, "I have it all right here, *Schwester*. It's hard to believe, but Mr. and Mrs. Hatfield are definitely not the people we thought they were."

The sheriff hung up the phone and Anna passed the paper over to him. "Sheriff, we have more evidence right here from the Decatur Daily paper. That's Mr. and Mrs. Hatfield right there."

Beth interrupted, "And that's their adopted daughter. The article says she went missing. That can't be a coincidence, right?"

The sheriff looked over at the deputy. He had just put down his cellphone. "Nothing yet, Sheriff, but they're gonna keep looking and call me back."

"Well, we better get out to the Hatfield's place and ask them some questions, Deputy. I'm gonna need you to go with me this time, so let's lock up." The sheriff then turned to the women and Moses, "Thank you so much for all of your help, but we've got to take it from here. Please go home and be safe. And let's just keep all of this a secret until we know more. If you hear anything else, let me know. I'll be around to let you know what I find out."

Beth, Anna and Moses gathered their things and exited the office. The three of them gathered in by their parked buggies for a short quiet prayer together before heading home. They prayed for safety for the sheriff and the deputy. They prayed for answers for the Packers and for the rest of the community. And they prayed for any necessary forgiveness for the Hatfields.

Chapter Twenty

The sheriff and the deputy pulled up at the Hatfield house, parking just off to the side of the mailbox. There were colorful flowers everywhere - some in pots on the porch, others were expertly landscaped, and even more cascading out of window boxes. The front door was painted a beautiful turquoise blue with a brass doorknob and matching knocker. The house itself was a light yellow with stark white shutters. From the outside, everything seemed perfect.

As the sheriff and deputy were stepping out of the cruiser, the deputy spotted a stream of smoke from the backyard and exclaimed, "Sheriff! There's a fire around back!"

The two ran on a brick path lined by trimmed hedges around the side of the house and laid eyes on Mr. Hatfield nursing a large bonfire in the center of his backyard. Laying on the ground next to the fire looked like a brand new twin mattress and a pile of bedding.

"Is he about to burn up the evidence?" muttered the sheriff, quietly. He motioned for the deputy to stay where he was at and watch the front of the house. He took a step out from the side of the house into Mr. Hatfield's view and called out, "Mr. Hatfield?"

Mr Hatfield looked up and instantly lost all color in his face. He didn't move, and he couldn't speak.

"Hi there, Mr. Hatfield," the sheriff spoke as he continued to approach Henry and the fire. He had one hand resting lightly on the butt of his gun that sat in his holster. "It's Sheriff Streen. I'm not sure we've met."

Mr. Hatfield remained motionless and silent. His shoulders were hunched over and his arms hung by his sides like limp noodles.

The sheriff continued. "I'm just here to ask a few questions, Mr. Hatfield. What d'ya say we go inside and chat?" As he stepped closer, he saw a tear fall down Mr. Hatfield's cheek and land on the top of his navy blue polo shirt, just above the pocket. "Are you okay, Mr. Hatfield? Let's go sit down."

Henry Hatfield just barely nodded his head and then turned slowly toward the house. The sheriff quickly pushed the mattress and the pink polka dot sheets and matching comforter away from the fire with his foot before following Mr. Hatfield into the back door of his home.

They walked through the kitchen and into the dining room. There were packed boxes lined up along the walls on either side of the windows. Through the large front window, the sheriff could see the deputy standing on the side porch. The living room furniture was wrapped in plastic, and from the dining room vantage point, the sheriff could see more boxes were pushed behind the sofa.

Mr. Hatfield sat down at the head of the table and rested his elbows on the table. His fingers were tightly interlaced and his hands were visibly shaking.

"Where's your wife, Mr. Hatfield?" the sheriff asked first.

Mr. Hatfield remained silent, staring ahead, tears now falling at a steady rate.

"Mr. Hatfield, do you want to tell me why you're upset right now?" the sheriff continued. He was pretty confident at this point that Mr. Hatfield was guilty, but he needed a confession.

"It's not what you think." Henry blurted out the words as if he had been holding his breath for too long. And with the words finally released, he began to sob. He held his face in his hands, his shoulders moving in rhythm with his quick breaths. "I know you think I killed Ruby Packer," he managed to utter, his voice trembling.

When the sheriff realized he wasn't going to say anything else, he said, "Did you kidnap Ruby Packer, Mr. Hatfield?"

Henry didn't answer, but he didn't need to. Right as he asked, Mrs. Hatfield came running into the room from the side hallway, screaming her husband's name. Sheriff Streen pulled his weapon and the deputy quickly entered through the front door, weapon in hand, as well.

Shirley Hatfield was a tall thin woman with a sharp long nose and thin lips. She wore her mousy brown hair in a short blunt haircut. Her voice was shrill as she screamed, "Henry! Don't you dare say anything! You didn't kill that girl! They can't prove anything!" She reached into her skirt pocket.

The sheriff yelled out, "Stop right there! Don't move! Both of you put your hands in the air!"

Henry looked up with a look of terror as he saw the sheriff's gun pointed at Shirley and the deputy's gun pointed at himself. He raised his arms into the air. "She has nothing to do with this," his voice pleaded to the sheriff but his eyes were panicked and focused on his wife. "Please, you don't understand."

At that moment, Shirley pulled a small .22 gun out of her pocket but before she could even point it forward, the sheriff fired a shot into her shoulder. Henry screamed out, "NO!" but it was a few seconds too late. Shirley screamed and fell backward. Her head fell perfectly positioned as if she were resting on the rolled up braided carpet that she had bought from the farmers' market just a month before. "You shot me!" Her voice sounded like the screech of an injured parakeet, small and harmless.

Henry jumped up sending his chair flying backwards, instinctively wanting to rush to her side, but the sheriff spoke loud and stern, "Sit. Down." The deputy had collected the .22 pistol with his handkerchief, his hands noticeably shaking, careful to not touch it and leave his own fingerprints on it anywhere.

"Deputy, call 911. Let them know we have two 10-15s. And we may need backup. We're taking these two in and I want to search the place and collect the evidence out back for DNA testing. Make sure that fire is put out, too." The sheriff said without taking his eyes off of Mr. Hatfield.

Mrs. Hatfield laid on the floor groaning and clinging to her arm, "I'm bleeding," she said with a high-pitched whine.

"Stay still," the sheriff said. "The ambulance is on its way." Shirley sat up, her face bright red. The sheriff instructed Deputy Brown to handcuff her one arm to the leg of the china cabinet next to her. The deputy fumbled but managed to secure Mrs. Hatfield. He stood up with weak knees and looked over at the sheriff. Sheriff Streen nodded at him in approval, and he headed out back to make his phone calls and extinguish the bonfire.

Once outside, Chase took a deep breath. He felt his heart racing. Now that he had stepped away, he was feeling overwhelmed with emotion and found himself working hard to fight back tears. As he approached the fire, he saw the pile of bedding. Everything still looked brand new. He would never again buy a new set of sheets without thinking about the ugliness of all of this. He couldn't imagine how scared poor beautiful Ruby must have felt while she was in captivity with these crazy people, and for the first time, he was doubting his decision to pursue the life of a deputy.

Was he cut out for this type of work? He tried desperately to stay focused as he started to make his phone calls.

Chapter Twenty-One

Sheriff Streen sat across from Henry Hatfield at the Lawson police station. Lawson was the closest city in Mainstay County with a full size operation, so Mr. Hatfield had been taken there for custody and for his trial. Sheriff Streen had asked if he could spearhead the interrogation and try to get a confession from him. Although the police were pretty confident they could use DNA evidence from the bedding and the mattress that were collected from the Hatfield property to confirm that Ruby was held hostage there until she died - they still didn't have the full story.

After some rest and knowing what he was up against, Henry had agreed to talk to Sheriff Streen. Shirley Hatfield had been treated in the hospital and was also being held at the Lawson jail. She was staying quiet and was waiting to speak to her attorney.

"We weren't able to have children of our own. Shirley and I. But after years of trying and waiting, we were finally chosen to adopt a perfect little girl. She was a baby, just over one-year-old when they brought her to us. Her name was Iris, like the flower. We were living in Decatur then, and we were so happy. I just knew that we were going to be happy forever." Mr. Hatfield paused and looked up at the sheriff. His eyes were dark and dull. "But that's not how life works."

The sheriff nodded, checking to make sure the recorder light was still shining red, indicating that the conversation was being recorded. Henry had agreed. He knew what he did was wrong. He just wanted to put it all behind him, do his time and live a different life. He hoped that cooperating with the police would allow for some leniency when it came to deciding his fate. Most importantly, he wanted everyone to know that he wasn't a killer. He never meant to hurt anyone.

"When Iris was almost twelve years old, we decided to get away and take a family camping trip. We rented an RV, and we took a cross-country trip out to the Pacific Northwest. The beaches were beautiful there. We had stayed a couple nights in a few different RV parks along the Oregon coast, but then I suggested to Shirley and Iris that we try to rough it one night. I had surprised them with a tent that I had packed away in one of the outer compartments of the camper rental. Iris was so excited. Her favorite book was about a family of three that went backpacking and camping. She had been telling me and Shirley all about how the family ate freeze-dried meals for dinner and oatmeal over a propane stove for breakfast. I wanted to do something like that for her, so we decided to park the RV and backpack out into the mountains and set up camp at a lake."

Henry stopped to take a sip of water from the water bottle that Mark had offered him. His stomach turned as he remembered leaving the same brand of bottled water on Ruby's bedside table in his basement just days earlier. He took a deep breath and continued, "Anyway, things went wrong, and something terrible happened to Iris. It was an accident, and we lost her. We were never the same after that, Shirley and me."

Sheriff Streen wanted to ask what happened, but knew it was best to let Henry continue telling his story. He was seeking closure on Ruby's case. It was clear that there was some history here, but he would happily leave that to the detectives.

Henry slumped forward in his chair. He leaned over, his hands clasped together in his lap and his upper arms pushing against the edge of the table. "We loved Iris more than anything. You have to believe that. But, we were scared that we were going to get blamed for her death. And it was already hard for us to lose her. So, we went home." He put his head in his hands. "We went home without her and reported her missing. We even offered a reward. No one ever found her, I don't think."

The sheriff was having a hard time keeping quiet. He drew in a slow breath and checked again to make sure the red light was still blinking on the recorder.

"So, that's how it all started," Henry continued. "Then, the next chapter begins with my marriage suffering. Shirley started to blame me for Iris's death, and she would say really mean things. I think she began to hate me, but I needed her. She was all I had left. So, I tried to fix things. That's all. But every time I tried, something would go wrong. Ruby was gonna be my last try, I promise."

Henry took another sip and fell quiet. The sheriff spoke, "Tell me about Ruby, Henry. Why did you pick her?"

Henry's mood seemed to change slightly as he sat up straighter. A small smile showed on his face as he began again. "The first time I saw Ruby was when I was watering the flowers outside my shop in Little Valley. Her face glowed like an angel and her eyes shone in the light. She looked so much like Iris - more than anyone else - and I think she was just a year older than Iris was. So, it seemed like we could pick up right where we left off."

Sheriff stifled the shiver he felt run down his spine.

Henry continued, staring past the sheriff as if he were talking to someone standing behind him. "I heard her girlfriend say her name, and I knew it was fate. You see, Shirley's birthday is in late July and her birthstone is the ruby. I know it wasn't her birthday, but I thought Shirley would still be so excited when she saw her and found out her name."

Henry's face changed. His eyebrows furrowed. "But, she wasn't excited. She's never happy. I worked so hard to give her Ruby. I studied her patterns without her knowing. I followed her a few times out to the woods. That boy she met was often late - she honestly deserved much better - but one day, he was late. And I was prepared. I finally had my chance. I grabbed her and took her home." Henry stopped and looked directly in the sheriff's eyes and said, "I didn't hurt her. I had bought a fancy new bed and a pretty new bed set so she could be comfortable."

The sheriff nodded. "What happened to her, Henry? What happened to Ruby?" He asked, working hard to keep a kind and trusting tone.

Henry looked away again. "It's always something, I swear. Like I said, Shirley wasn't happy. I think it's because Ruby was Amish, but I can't be sure. Anyway, we had an argument, and I swore I was gonna return her. But then, I came down to bring her dinner, and she said she wasn't feeling well. I thought it was a trick, but even if she was sick, how was I supposed to take her to the doctor?" Again, his eyes met the sheriff's, pleading for understanding. He continued, "Anyway, I came back upstairs and asked Shirley what we should do if Ruby was really sick. She said I 'made my bed, now deal with it.' The next morning, I brought Ruby breakfast, and she was dead." He took in a quick breath. "I guess she was telling the truth. Ruby told me she had epilepsy, but I didn't know that. I thought she was making it up. I was gonna let her go, I swear." He repeated those words again, but this time, his voice sounded childlike and his eyes were cast down at the table.

The sheriff clenched his hands into fists under the table. He felt like he probably had heard enough and didn't want to give this guy another minute of his time, but Henry continued. "She looked so beautiful and peaceful. I knew she loved the woods, so I just brought her back where I grabbed her and figured that the boyfriend might get blamed for it. I panicked."

The sheriff had heard enough. He needed a break. "I think that's all we need today, Henry," he said as he motioned for the door to be opened.

Henry stood up. "You gotta believe me that I didn't kill her, Sheriff. I was gonna let her go, I swear!" Henry begged for understanding as the police officer fastened handcuffs on Henry.

Sheriff Mark Streen was speechless. He opened his mouth but he couldn't think of anything to say. And maybe that was for the better. He remembered his mother telling him years ago that "some things are just better left unsaid" and he'd never found a more fitting time to apply that little phrase.

He placed his cowboy hat on his head and walked out of the room ahead of Henry. He wanted to get back to his new home in Little Valley and tell the Packers, and the twins, the deputy, and everyone else, that the case was officially solved. The bad guys were locked away, and the town was safe and sound again.

And he was going to do whatever he could to keep it that way.

Chapter Twenty-Two

"Could you please pass the butter, *Schwester*?" Anna said. Beth reached over and picked up the china butter dish and handed it to Sarah who handed it to Moses. Eli and Noah sat at the heads of the large rectangular table in Anna's open dining area. Anna sat to the right of her husband, Eli, while Beth sat to the right of her husband, Noah. Matthew shared the side of the table with Beth, and Sarah and Moses shared Anna's side of the table. Sarah's two young children were playing quietly in the living room. They had finished their dinner earlier and would join the adults for dessert.

Sarah's youngest child, Rosemary, had finally fallen asleep in her arms. Beth offered to take her to the bassinet. When Beth returned to the table, Sarah said, "We have so much to celebrate tonight, my *wunderbarr* family."

"*Ach ja*, indeed, we do, daughter," Anna responded. As she finished spreading butter on her roll, she reached for the roll on Eli's plate to do the same. The twins had cooked together to prepare their favorite chicken and dressing dinner. Sarah had boiled green beans from the freezer and seasoned them beautifully, and of course, the sisters added fresh homemade baked rolls to the night's menu. A glass pitcher of iced meadow tea with slices of frozen lemon floating on top served as the centerpiece to the dinner.

Beth chimed in, "We can all sleep so much better now that we have a *gut* sheriff and deputy team in Little Valley."

"That's true," said Sarah, "not to mention a couple pretty smart investigators in our own little community." She winked at Anna. Beth grinned and nodded.

"We can thank *Gotte* that our Anna and Beth are safe," Noah said, squeezing Beth's hand. "Maybe it's time to take a break from police work for a while," he said, setting his fork down and looking directly in Beth's face.

Anna exclaimed, "I second that!" Beth rolled her eyes, and laughter rose into the air above the table filling the room with warmth. "And we can thank *Gotte* that my cane... as beautiful as it is... is retired next to the fireplace now, and that my knee has fully healed."

"Amen" said Sarah, Beth and Eli in unison.

"And Matthew, you have some *gut* news to share, too, eh?" Moses asked, encouraging him to share.

All eyes were on Matthew when he said, "*Ja,* it's true. It's exciting, indeed. Just before the arrest, I had closed a deal with the Hatfields to purchase the flower shop. They had asked me to keep it a secret until after they had moved, which I thought was strange, but now I guess it all makes sense..."

"Congratulations, Matt!" Eli reached out and gave Matthew's arm a light pat. "That's *wunderbarr* news! You and Moses will be *nochbers*!"

"*Ja,* I am so excited for our *schtores* to be right next to each other. Sarah will have to make two lunches now every day," Moses nudged Sarah with a grin.

"*Ja,* no problem. I've got all the time in the world," said Sarah, laughing.

"What will you name your new *schtore,* Matthew?" Beth asked.

Matthew paused, "I'm not sure. I'm open to suggestions, if anyone has one. Beiler's Flowers doesn't sound too *gut,* I don't think. "

Anna and Beth looked at each other and said in unison, "The Secret Garden!"

Sarah and the men burst into laughter. "That's perfect!" Sarah exclaimed.

Anna and Beth smiled at one another from opposite corners of the table. Without speaking, they knew that moving away was no longer on the agenda. Little Valley was their home, and their family was too important to leave behind.

"The Secret Garden, it is," said Matthew, his face beamed.

Noah raised his glass into the air, and everyone followed suit. "*Gotte* is *gut*! A toast to health, happiness, and success!"

The family cheered, "For sure and certain!"

The peace and quiet doesn't last long in Little Valley as the Amish community faces big changes and big threats with tourism booming. It appears as if some of the new businesses want control of the market, and it looks like they are willing to go to great lengths to get it.. With one barn after another set on fire in the middle of the night, it becomes personal, and the community is scared for the well-being of their families and their future in the small town. Anna and Beth jump in to untangle the clues and find the culprits behind the fires. In Saving Grace, the pressure is on as it comes down to the two of them to convince the community that Little Valley is the town they want to continue to call home.

Saving Grace is the third (and next!) book in the Amish Lantern Mystery Series. Visit my website at **marybbarbee.com** to grab your copy!

Is your mouth watering after reading all about those delicious Amish treats? Well, I have a gift for you! Visit **marybbarbee.com/ALMS-cookbook** to get instant access to *The Amish Lantern Mystery Series Cookbook*. Inside, you'll find Anna and Beth's Amish Apple Butter Cakelets with Caramel Sauce, Amish Meadow Tea, and Amish Butterscotch Cinnamon Rolls recipes... and so much more, including a few extra flavorful recipes that are introduced later in the Amish Lantern Mystery Series.

Acknowledgments

---•◦•---

This book wouldn't be complete without a page dedicated to the gratitude I feel towards all the help, love and support I get throughout the writing process.

Thank you to all my friends and family for showering me with support. For not only buying the first book in the series, but also sharing honest wonderful feedback to keep in mind while writing this next story. I am overwhelmed with gratitude for all of you and am dedicated to giving back just as much as I receive from each of you.

Thank you to my new readers, especially to all of you who have written such heart-warming emails. I absolutely love reading every single email I receive, and I made a point to implement some of your stories and experiences into this book in hopes that it brings a little bit more mystery and excitement as you read it.

As always, thank you to my mother, Molly Misko, my Christian inspiration, my expert beta reader and content editor. Without her, these books would lack insight, creativity and would most definitely have a grammatical error or two.

And to my dear friend, Jenny Raith, how do I put this into words? Not only is she the first blogger to brag about the Amish Lantern Mystery Series, but she is also a big piece of the brainstorming that goes into each story and the editing that helps push it out onto the shelves.

Thank you to my daughter, Laura Fry, for always suggesting where I could add more imagery and most importantly, for filling my life – and edits – with humor.

Finally, I must give thanks to my sister, Julie Rietze, who I swear is my twin born two years early. She joined the editing team for this book, stepping in to help last minute and proving to be pretty awesome at finding even the smallest mistake. I'm pretty sure she could quite possibly serve as my life coach, too.

– and for all of this, I am forever grateful.

A Note From the Author

Thank you so much for reading *Secrets in Little Valley*. This book was a true labor of love, with many more edits than the first. I thoroughly enjoy the process of writing, and this book was certainly no exception.

Right off the bat, I struggled with the idea of "killing off" Ruby. What is a murder mystery without an untimely death, though, right?

If I had to pick a favorite new character, Sheriff Streen would be an easy choice. I fought back tears while writing the heavy conversation he had with the Packers' in Chapter 10. I hope you felt how he managed that with much needed compassion.

I was so excited to bring Sarah and Moses back into this story and to introduce Moses' childhood friend, Matthew. I was equally excited to introduce a few more villains into the story, as well.

Chase's storyline was written and rewritten a number of times. There was much debate among my beta readers and editors over whether Chase should be attracted to young Ruby or not, but that's how the story unfolded in my mind. Instead of a creepy side of that, I hoped for the takeaway and the focus to be about Ruby – she was certainly a special girl.

Overall, the most treasured parts of this book are definitely the Amish recipes and the pieces that tell a bit more about my favorite twin sisters, Anna and Beth.

I can't wait for you to read what happens next! Want to be notified when my next book releases? Visit my website at marybbarbee.com to sign up for my new release email list.

Thank you again for choosing *Secrets in Little Valley* to add to your book selection. If you enjoyed it, please consider leaving a review on Goodreads or Bookbub – or by simply recommending it to a friend!

With so much gratitude,

Mary B. Barbee

About the Author

---✦---

Mary B. Barbee is the author of the *Amish Lantern Mystery Series*. As an avid fan of all mystery and suspense in print, on television and in film, Mary B. believes the best mystery is one where the suspect changes throughout the story, keeping the audience guessing. She enjoys providing an exciting escape for a few hours with stories her readers can't put down - and always with a surprise ending.

When not writing, Mary B. is either playing a couple sets of tennis or a strategy board game with her two witty daughters and her kindly competitive mother. The four of them share a home in the Inland Northwest in the beautiful town of Spokane, Washington with their really cute - but sometimes naughty - chihuahua.

Mary B. loves to hear from her readers. Connect at:

marybbarbee@gmail.com

www.facebook/marybbarbee

Instagram @marybbarbee

www.marybbarbee.com

More Books to Read By Mary B. Barbee

THE AMISH LANTERN MYSTERY SERIES

Thick As Thieves – Book 1

Robberies are running rampant in Little Valley, and the quiet small-town lives of the Amish community are suddenly thrown into chaos.

Secrets in Little Valley – Book 2

With the bishop's daughter suddenly missing and a new sheriff in town, Anna and Beth find themselves roped into solving another mystery in their small town.

Saving Grace – Book 3

The Amish community in Little Valley is facing big changes, and big threats, with tourism booming. It becomes clear that some of the new businesses want control of the market, and it looks like they are willing to go to great lengths to get it.

Good Intentions – Book 4

Hazel Thompson is found dead in Little Valley's now-famous Amish Inn, and there's a long list of suspects with plenty of motive.

A Blessing in Disguise – Book 5

Jessica McLean opens shop to find a man has been left for dead on the floor of her diner. Could the crime could be related to Jessica's new relationship with their beloved Matthew Beiler?

Christmas Chaos in Little Valley - Book 6

Beth finds out that the Little Valley library is shutting its doors due to a lack of funding and very disturbing anonymous threats.

THE ABIGAIL BAKER MYSTERY SERIES
Blind Faith — Prequel

Abigail's excitement for her new home is replaced by doom and gloom when she finds out that an unexplained murder has rocked the residents of her new town. And not unusual to her, it's the Amish community that is suspect number one.

**Grab your free e-copy of Blind Faith at:
marybbarbee.com/blindfaith**

Where Fear Ends — Book 1

A town councilman is found dead by the side of the road in the Amish community of Abigail Baker's new hometown.

A Multitude of Sins — Book 2

When secret notes containing serious threats are unveiled, Abigail wonders if the latest victim could have been hiding a multitude of sins.

A Wing and a Prayer – Book 3 ~ COMING SOON!

THE PUPCAKE MYSTERY SERIES
Cupcakes and Corruption – Prequel
Battling empty-nest syndrome, Eliza finds solace in the company of her adorable chihuahua, Pupcake, and her dreams of opening a quaint coffee shop. Little does she know that her talent for baking and nurturing also extends to amateur sleuthing.
Grab your free e-copy of Cupcakes and Corruption at:
marybbarbee.com/pupcakeprequel

Sweet Suspicion – Book 1
The charming town of Copeland is buzzing with excitement as Eliza and her adorable chihuahua, Pupcake, open their new coffee shop. But when a body is discovered on

the premises, the duo must put down their baking tools and pick up their detective hats.

Confections and Clues – Book 2 – Coming Valentine's Day 2025

Eliza and Pupcake's lakeside getaway takes a dark turn when they stumble upon a body. With a secretive small town and a case no one wants solved, Eliza's sweet retreat quickly turns into another mystery. Can she and Pupcake crack the case before the killer's trail goes cold?

Recipe for Reckoning – Book 3 ~ COMING SOON!

Find excerpts, purchase links and more at
www.marybbarbee.com